Distance No Object

Distance No Object

Stories by Gloria Frym

City Lights Books
San Francisco

Cover design by Big Fish
Book design by James Brook
Typography by Harvest Graphics
Cover photograph © 1999 by Richard Misrach, courtesy Fraenkel Gallery,
    San Francisco
Author photograph © 1999 by Michael Aron

Some of these stories have appeared in slightly different versions in *Anatomy
Raw, Blind Date, Exquisite Corpse, Gare du Nord, Longshot, Caprice, New American
Writing, Processed World,* and *First Intensity.*
        The author is deeply grateful to Ruth Morgan, James Brook, and David
Rompf for their generous readings of this work, and the Fund for Poetry for
angelic support.

Library of Congress Cataloging-in-Publication Data

Frym, Gloria.
        Distance no object / by Gloria Frym.
            p.   cm.
        ISBN 0-87286-358-1 (pbk.)
        1. Berkeley (Calif.) — Social life and customs Fiction.   2. City and
    town life—California—Berkeley Fiction.   I. Title.
    PS3556.R95D57   1999
    813'.54—dc21   99-34686
                                                                            CIP

City Lights Books are available to bookstores through our primary distributor:
Subterranean Company, P. O. Box 160, 265 S. 5th St., Monroe, OR 97456.
541-847-5274. Toll-free orders 800-274-7826. FAX 541-847-6018. Our books
are also available through library jobbers and regional distributors. For personal
orders and catalogs, please write to City Lights Books, 261 Columbus Avenue,
San Francisco, CA 94133. Visit our web site: www.citylights.com

CITY LIGHTS BOOKS are edited by Lawrence Ferlinghetti and Nancy J.
Peters and published at the City Lights Bookstore, 261 Columbus Avenue,
San Francisco, CA 94133

for Julia, again

Count not that far that can be had,
Though sunset lie between—
Nor that adjacent, that beside,
Is further than the sun.

—Emily Dickinson, #1074

Contents

"To See Her in Sunlight Was to See Marxism Die"

First love is exactly like a revolution; the regular and established order of life is in an instant smashed to fragments; youth stands at the barricade, its bright banner raised high in the air, and sends its ecstatic greetings to the future, whatever it may hold—death or a new life, no matter.
  —Turgenev, *The Torrents of Spring*

AT THE END of the Russian movie *Burnt by the Sun,* my husband burst into tears. We had been estranged, but when the credits came on, I got up from my seat and he got up from his and we held each other closely for one of the last times.

You could say that many years of knowing each other—the last few of which were a lot like the death of international socialism and the parallel meltdown of the Soviet Union and all that it once mythically promised—no matter how it executed those promises, no matter how reality never lives up to dream—you could say that the death of our ideals left us open to this now exceptional display of emotion.

The whole thing burned too brightly and people—individual and particular people—suffered and died.

By the time Russia was only Russia again, idealism, not to mention romance, was in an international decline.

Once my husband hired a chamber ensemble to serenade me for my birthday. Now his taste in music struck me as sentimental, especially his affection for the drawing-room rhythms of Haydn.

When we were poor and sweet with each other, the day I got laid off my first real job we took the ferry by moonlight from the Berkeley Marina to San Francisco. He hailed a taxi to Union Square where he indulged me in champagne at the St. Francis and a pair of expensive Italian shoes.

Much later, for a long time, the sound of his steps on the last splintery wooden stairs leading up to the porch filled me with dread.

During the several years of our demise, I would daydream about hurling his neatly arranged penny loafers, one pair after another, out of the room, out the door, down the steps. *Leave!* I would shriek, pounding the sole of the last shoe on the banister like Khrushchev pounded his shoe on the table during a summit conference. *Leave now while you can run, before it's too late!*

At the end of the Chekhovian *Burnt*, everything falls apart, and the lovely pastel summers on the veranda of the dacha among the artists and children, the fields so crowded with flowers and the lunches so long and languorous all come to an end. Jealous husband is carted off by secret police, betrayals surface and counter-betrayals surface and everybody is arrested, and the credits tell us that mostly everybody who was young and fresh and in love winds up detained or dying in Stalin's labor camps.

We had the big things in common, the big ideals outside ourselves—we believed in justice, equality, social change. It was only the little things, like who would wash the dishes, why a red wheelbarrow instead of the green one he settled for, or when to pay the bills—the daily negotiables that over time add up two lives and make the sum a lot larger than its constituents. It was the little disagreements that bankrupted our romance, like so many unrecorded withdrawals.

And then trapped in the deficit, we began to look like empty, overdrawn silhouettes of our parents, even after years of protesting otherwise,

The little things really contain the secret to a counterintelligence that lives inside each one of us and functions simultaneously to the authorized intelligence and participates in a countereconomy, etc. It's the little things that corrupt the big, theoretical principles, and not the other way around.

He had a little black market going too, on the side, for a long time.

My husband was lucky, though. I resolutely revered mind over matter. I was not a materialist in love or in vengeance. I knew of another wife, who upon discovering conclusive evidence of her husband's betrayal, flung open the door to his closet and cut off one leg of every pair of pants he owned. The amputated heaped and hanging—at last separate and equal.

Yes, the little things accrue in a domestic life, like stones brought by slaves to make the pyramids, and pretty soon, two formerly autonomous sovereigns find themselves in a tomb they built together, with no visible mortar.

"We will bury you!" Nikita Khrushchev howled at Richard Nixon. But Krushchev died first, a man stripped of his dignity, and Nixon went out as an official hero in some people's eyes.

Mere days after we moved into a pretty house in a good neighborhood, safe, we assumed, from the gunshot and degradation of our old block, my husband and I were sitting around too tired to unpack.

We both had lots of leftover countercultural reservations about this new house. Our bad old neighborhood was a political decision, we had told ourselves. For a decade, we lived in terror of crossing the street at night just because we thought it was too bourgeois to live elsewhere.

"Is it too grand?" I asked him as we drove by the day we signed the papers. The house sat, somewhat imperiously, on the cusp of a hill street reminiscent of a Tuscan village, and for that, its location signaled an upward mobility our incomes didn't actually support. But we did it anyway, graduating from our cash-only lives, floating loans left and right, like other good American debtors. Japanese maples lined the walk to the public school our child would attend. The bay sparkled in the distance through giant pines and redwoods and live oaks. The house was beautiful and architecture is a kind of destiny, I argued.

I thought beauty would have mercy on us, that we could crowd ourselves with it and our selves would dissolve in its greater radiance or merge in the face of collective victory.

Okay, the marriage was dying, and like Gorbachev's *Perestroika*, I made some rash, spendthrift moves to open trade to the West, for which I would be reviled in years to come and which would contribute to our rapid downfall.

But why not enjoy beauty while you're dying? A question I took for granted at the time.

I had just smoked a joint. It was bad enough I had smoked alone and read the first paragraph of every article in a recent

Scientific American which I could not understand but which I thought sounded quite mellifluous.

We weren't fighting, were absent-mindedly knarling about something. In marriage, such low-level complaint is a form of expressing ideals—ideals that in our case used to be reserved for foreign policy and that do not translate well domestically.

Which cupboard to put the cups in. I'm left-handed and he's always accused me of setting up a left-handed kitchen, what with my flea-market leftovers and odd collection of memorial candle glasses we never used for juice like I always insisted we would when I wouldn't throw them out. What can I say, that's the way I am. And among two people, this could be a terrible thing.

"We should get divorced some time," he casually let out.

I wondered what he meant.

"Whaaaat did you say?" I said. The TV was blaring as it usually did when he was trying to relax. This was not my idea of leisure. He had been vying for cable, but I was terrified of having sixty-five channels breathing the same air. His announcement sounded like something he had just heard on a sitcom, so I let out some canned laughter.

"I mean, we should, you know, I mean. . . ."

This was it, this was how he told me of his oppression. He didn't, couldn't repeat the d-word. Not even a quiet bloodless coup, just dribs and drabs, leaky-faucet style. I myself remained dry-eyed incredulous. In the ensuing weeks, the toilet kept flushing itself over and over in the downstairs subcode bathroom. I would have to get a plumber to tell me it was hopeless to fix.

You might suppose I was some hotshot Marxist. That I'd read and studied and that my wired-rimmed glasses really counted for something. No, *he* was the kind of guy who on a beach vacation in

Mexico would take along *The Essential Works of Marx,* not me. What I knew about Marxism you could put in a teacup, but I was one of those believers without much need for evidence, swept up in the romance of a grand social theory that sounded better than any political and economic system I was living in.

At first I had been leery of theory, disliking it as Marianne Moore said she disliked poetry. But reading it, with a perfect contempt for it, I had begun to discover in it a place for the genuine. It began to strike me as poetry, but maybe that was all the dope.

There was no predicting what you didn't know, was there? And what we didn't know at twenty or twenty-five, but sensed as righteously as our youth would allow, was that Vietnam, that thorny symbol of all that separated us from everything that came before us, would be the theoretical and actual bedrock of our collective imaginations. Would actually dictate whether or not we felt guilty about having a nice house twenty years later.

We were seeds strewn by that war, transplanted to a place where there were others of our kind, albeit not exactly re-seeding ourselves. Though other wars followed, they weren't ours. Even our protest of them was a pale simulation of our early and historical passion.

For a long time after our union disintegrated, I walked around North Berkeley like a grim peasant in a dark babushka, lips firmly set together in semi-permanent sadness. I would wait in those lively bread lines at the Cheese Board and the Juice Bar, utterly failing to appreciate the last worker-owned collectives of my village. The rug of a bad political system had been pulled out from beneath me, and the economy inside had collapsed with it. Let's just say I fell apart from devastation and shortage. And stayed apart for the years after his announcement when he couldn't actually bring himself to leave. A day would see me spiraling into ferocious thoughts, misdirected at anyone in sight, such as the long-haired gardener next door, stupidly pruning a wall of double-flowering, crimson bougainvillea in the middle of July. I shrieked at him like a crazed war widow, ran back into the house and slammed the door and got into bed. Did I imagine I could control anything on earth?

When my husband moved out, he took almost nothing and, as a kind of vindication, he left his shoes neatly lined up across the entrance to his small study. I let out the breath I had been holding for years and went about my business. There was nothing to recover or patch, only the usual arrangements to be negotiated, and the future, gratefully uncertain. I never liked the unpoetic certainty of marriage anyway, looming there outside of two people and their thoughts like a stop sign. It was suddenly spring, though it had been spring for several months, and the light high and thin reflected off the bay, bathing the blue marguerites and delphiniums that faithfully sprang up among the grasses in what used to be the garden. During the protracted period of my marital dissolution, I had long ceased to care for plants, I had in fact developed a certain contempt for my own touch. My anger was so tinged with melancholy and yet so volatile that I thought it might pollute the very soil in which long-standing perennials reappeared yearly, indifferent to human betrayal.

There was our growing child to attend to, and we both naturally worried about her reaction to the breakup. We each worshiped her and tried not to treat her like a satellite. How would she fare in this new separate-but-equal liberation struggle? How would she react to my future free-market economy?

One afternoon, I stared out at her through an open window as she spoke to a companion only she could see. Then she leapt into the brush in her black leotards and pink fairy wings, her cheeks flushed, a magic wand in one hand and a rope in the other as though she were out to lasso whatever creature or force she determined to invoke. The gold star at the end of her wand sparkled in the sun.

I grabbed the small automatic camera my husband had left behind and tried to focus, but it was too simple — how could I get her square in the middle of the frame, light behind her, without adjusting the absent f-stop? I fiddled with the zoom, and she appeared closer and closer, though she was not closer than she appeared. How miraculous late-capitalist technology!

She danced, she raised her arms toward the heavens, she whipped her rope around, she touched the blue marguerites with her magic wand. I began to shoot, wildly, as wildly as an automatic camera allows a mother at a long distance to shoot. Not with quite the same frenzy as the famous scene in *Blow Up,* but there she was on the grass in the sunlight with no idea someone was stealing her image, documenting her performance, creating evidence of a charmed childhood to trot out someday to a future suitor. I shot and I shot and I knew she would never be this way again, I knew that the dissolution of the marriage would change her in some profound fashion, and though it was only one of the many tragedies she would suffer, perhaps not even *the* tragedy of her life, there would be the inevitable and natural loss of her childhood, and that alone was enough to mourn.

And the damned tears rolled down my cheeks, blustery and overdue, and I didn't care and I didn't wipe them, for I was afraid she would suddenly stop playing and skip into the house, as children often do when they're called by a spirit that speaks only to them. I kept clicking pictures until the film would no longer advance, the button would no longer click.

Toward the end of a roll of film, it ought to say THE END, just like in the movies.

I am very happy now.

Tagging

A YEAR AFTER I moved out of the old bad neighborhood, my new garbage can was tagged.

It's not a can, of course, but a giant green monument to tough plastic, rigid and made to last forever. *Container designed for ordinary domestic refuse only,* warns the lid. *Do not load with liquids, chemicals, ashes or other flammable, toxic or hazardous materials. Do not overload with sand, soil, rocks or other heavy materials. Do not place on elevated platform, steep slope or close to driveway.* I would never dream of dumping hot ashes from the hearth. I am the type of person who follows such instructions carefully, who follows most sorts of admonitions when they are written in plain English.

The new neighborhood in North Berkeley had a park nearby, a lot of old trees, new birdlife, higher taxes. I shouldn't be coy about it. The house is definitely better digs and prettier and safer. Instead of a steady stream of nuts roaming around, there is a steady flow of automobile traffic, which tends to irritate the nerves in a much less personal way.

There was the occasional homeless person trudging up the hill to rummage around the cans and bottles we leave out for the recyclers. I don't really care who makes what on these items, only that they get to the proper place so that they, like Hindus, can enjoy their next lifetime. A mayonnaise jar may wind up elevated to a pitcher or demoted to a pimento container. Who can tell? Such is the will of whoever oversees these brief, brittle lives.

I knew from the day we moved into the house that our tenure was to be short-lived. At least our tenure as a family was soon to undergo nuclear fission. We were on our way out, we were about to violate the dominant paradigm known as family values, we were to dismantle and proceed with our fragmented, though not utterly atomized, lives.

But not before we underwent certain initiations.

A couple of very tall older women neighbors from slightly uphill wanted their view. They were willing to pay for it. They were therapists; they were divorcees in their late fifties who made good divorces many years ago and who got the houses, houses that were bought at the beginning of time. They had so much excess capital that between them they could pay a guy who claimed to have a master's degree in psychology to top and "window" all the trees downhill from them.

It seems the trees, fulsome refuges that they were for a variety of wildlife, stood in the way of Their Bay.

Of course, unlike the neighbors in my previous neighborhood who simply walked outside one morning and axed down the offending plum trees between our unfenced yards, these tall ladies demanded permission.

They arrived in turtlenecks and baggy blue jeans on their scouting mission. One held a clipboard and the other smiled, empty-handed.

"What sort of tree would you like to plant in the far corner of your yard, if you had your wish of wishes?" one of them asked me. "Of course, we'll contribute. . . ."

Cutting down full-grown branches of already perfectly good trees and denuding my view of these bare ruined choirs and offering cash replacement is a little like wiping a person's brow and stabbing them at the same time.

"Well, I," I said. "I'll have to think about it." I lied, knowing I wouldn't be living in this house long enough to wait out the growth of a sapling. Besides, we were comparatively poor, they were rich.

For them it was a *fait accompli*, but not for me. Windowing made the trees look anorexic and banished the birds, and I remembered what Thoreau said regarding all manner of commerce: *It's no good, if no birds sing there.*

They would not take no or even later for an answer and after several unpleasant letters full of soft sell like, *We were disappointed that you didn't respond*, etc., I received a letter from their attorney.

"Their attorney?" I laughed, as my husband informed me of a lawsuit.

"There's an ordinance, incomprehensible . . . and they've attached it to their letter."

About the tagging. It worried me. It was illegible, indecipherable, and the moment I spotted the chalky cuneiform on the belly of the can, I suspected a secret code, a signal to another world, from an unknown group that staked its claim when I slept.

You've seen walls above freeways tagged thick like murals, filled with mysterious orthography. You can imagine daredevil tightrope walking to get to these reaches, late at night, the blinding headlights of oncoming vehicles, the deafening swoosh as they speed past the writers who hang by one leg as they keep scrawling their unearthly bulletins. When you're very young, this is a thrill. When you're older, even imagining it is worse than the worst hangover.

This handwriting on the wall has been there for some time and it's not at all like KILROY WAS HERE. It doesn't declare, with a sort of levity, a kind of kiss-and-tell flight, it says something else, something potent and dangerous and sad, and it's a language whose syllables we can't enunciate, whose particulars we can't understand.

But we know it means something.

It kills us not to know.

"Go ahead, kill me," my husband glared, as I picked up a butcher knife to slice a cherry tomato.

I once almost had a fight with a painter friend, while we trudged up eight flights of stairs to her loft in a converted telephone company building in New York.

"Let's walk instead of waiting for the elevator," she said cheerfully. "It will be good exercise."

Her breathing got closer with every flight. The stairwells were covered with colorful graffiti.

"Look at this," she snickered, every other step.

"Don't you find the patterns mildly interesting, potentially inspiring?"

"They're filthy, disgusting, revolting, and how do these kids get in here?"

"But it's writing and it's trying to speak."

"You think this is writing? This is shit."

What she hated most of all was the New York art world selling this stuff in galleries and rich people buying it and hanging it on the white walls of their own living rooms.

You can never tell what people think is worth looking at. Another friend, a photographer, once made giant portraits of prison inmates, maximum-security inmates, whose bodies often seemed like scratch pads covered with ink. Whose rigid faces, whose pumped-up pecs and biceps didn't seem like dining or living room material to me. Who were the people who bought these artworks, who could sit down to a nice meal with bulging tattoos the size of musk melons so close to their plates?

I may not be the best purveyor of art.

I called my husband. "Hey," I said, "we've been tagged."

He chuckled. Chuckled is the sort of thing you do in our new neighborhood, the sort of thing you couldn't do with impunity in our old neighborhood. There was something about the gunfire and the bass of car stereos that prevented chuckling, even in private.

Wld you pls remember to pay the g-dm ins today. Do you want them to cncl r loan?

The tagging was one of several small assaults that occurred after our first year of residence. We were busy fighting and estranging ourselves from each other, preparing for the many years ahead of relatively good, if restrained, cheer between us as a separated couple. Something had to be misidentified and killed between us so that the good could return, and we went about ripping up our internal furniture with impulsive abandon. There was no arena of transgression that I personally did not dredge up, involuntarily, of course, during the heat of an argument. . . . *And you don't remember when you . . . you ALWAYS do that . . . and it's just symbolic of the whole problem between us . . . which is you simply don't want to . . . and will NEVER manage to . . . and I can't forgive you for . . .* and so on.

None of the things that happened in the new neighborhood happened in the old neighborhood where we began our slow moral descent. They were only two miles apart, but moving seemed to memorialize old crimes in new bottles.

How can I remember the arguments, they evaporated almost as soon as they occurred. The new house, older and darker than the old house, seemed to drag history out of us and prevented us from initiating new conciliatory actions toward each other yet encouraged us to hurl old infractions into the air and revive them with new breath. A Serbo-Croatian light hung about the house, tragic, autumnal, bellicose. One of us would heat up, start fuming and spitting. The words would skyrocket, like kites with fire-crackers on their tails, then they would disappear.

It is unforgivable and impermissible for you to use such language and yell at me in front of our child. If this is a scare tactic to get me to move, it is succeeding.

Of course, we had already been initiated with a variety of small crimes against our property. I always suspect an inside job. Neighbors no longer call the Welcome Wagon to deliver baked goods and tea cozies to new neighbors. According to the Berkeley police, people from presumably outside the neighborhood steal into the neighborhood early in the morning before the sun rises and break into cars to remove their stereos.

Or bust the locks on garages. Ours contained nothing but boxes piled up from the move. Mind you, we saved those boxes, because at least one of us truly believed he or she would be needing them for the impending move out. It must have been terribly disappointing to the thieves, not to find salable goods. I nearly felt sorry for them, felt like next time leaving a dish of milk or something, behind a tree.

The worst thing so far was the pumpkin. Someone, while we were out trick-or-treating, stole a giant pumpkin right off our front porch. You might think that both parents taking their only child trick-or-treating was rather perverse, considering that they could not get along in the same room. We did many such activities together. Neither of us wanted to miss a thing our child did, for we loved her with a passion that exceeded the contempt we then felt for one another.

The pumpkin wasn't carved, it was too big and too majestic to deface, I thought. It was the kind of pumpkin that took at least two people to move, so clearly the thief had an accomplice. Perhaps someone he felt contemptuous of but needed.

Nothing that has been stolen from me, not jewelry or computers or any other gadget, made me feel as sad as losing this pumpkin. Because I had to say to my little boy, "Honey, someone stole the pumpkin." And then he had to go to school the next day and tell everyone, "You Know What? Someone stole our pumpkin!"

It was low, it was mean, it was evil, on a night that make-believe demons are supposed to reign, and it was not funny.

This tagging. It was a message, it was written, and like all messages begged to be decoded, just like the secret writings of the Maya.

Pls tk yr fking laundry out of the bskt

someone wrote someone else at my house, scrawled impertinently in lipstick on the bathroom mirror.

The day after Valentine's, I found my first crack vial by the curb. I knew how to properly identify it because the *New Yorker* had an article about a guy who collected them from all over the country, and there was a color photo of them in a fancy display case facing the text.

"Look at that," I motioned to my husband as he was putting something into the passenger seat. "Looks like our virginity is gone."

"Well," he looked closer.

I'm myopic and he's farsighted.

"Well," he said in his usual droll tone. "Could be a glass holder from a single-stem red rose, couldn't it?"

"Yeah sure," I said. "The one you didn't bring me this year."

Canticle

AT THE BIRTHDAY PARTY in the park, the children were told to pair off for the water-balloon fight.

Early fall in Berkeley, three o'clock sun still warm enough for a swim. A dry heat not usual for this mild bay climate. Here summers frustrated the fruit, dampened off the tomatoes from their rightful sweetness, yet adored the flower. An autumn child entered life anticipating November rains, a short cool season, spring flirting by late January, with plum buds perfuming the misted nights almost before the leaves left the trees.

The moist grass left wet imprints on the seats of the childrens' pants, and when they got up to pair off, all fifteen dark patches nearly matched.

The boys paired off with the boys, the girls with the girls, except for one, a fat girl, older, taller than the others, bullied in the usual ways at school. Familiar taunts, always left alone. "She can be partners with herself," both boys and girls whispered.

The children did not dislike her, no, it simply did not occur to them to protect her. They knew nothing of her sufferings, she appeared self-sufficient.

Adults thought her helpful with younger children, anticipated her loneliness, kept offering cookies, believing in the good magic of sweet treats which they knew was a bad magic, was the magic they used to keep her allied to them, they who also used this magic on themselves.

Now the pairs of children tossed water balloons to one another, a missed catch drenching a partner, knocking him or her out of the game. Soon only a few singles were left throwing balloons; they became bored and wandered back to the picnic table for sodas or dispersed into small, noisy groups on the peripheries of the grass.

The cutting of the birthday cake drew the party together in a circle, at center the birthday boy and his mother, and two other mothers who volunteered to supervise the games. Eight candles were lit, the flames stood straight up toward the breezeless sky. The cake was decorated like a baseball diamond, topped with a figurine of a baseball boy in old-fashioned knickers, something out of baseball's childhood, a fringe of blond hair peeking out of his cap, a slight blush on his cheeks.

"Who wants to go for a nice refreshing swim after all that birthday cake?" one mother asked. She looked around at faces smudged with icing, crumpled napkins, and paper cups.

"Could be your last chance till next summer," she said.

The children giggled. The mother looked puzzled. She had not thought she said anything very funny. Was it too soon to swim, she wondered, do they think they have to wait an hour after eating? Several girls obediently got up to look for their towels. The boys were herded to a nearby plum tree where another mother was hoisting up a donkey-shaped piñata by its neck.

"You all know how to play this?" the mother asked cheerfully, handing one boy a bat.

"Yeeeesss," the children dragged out the word as though mocking her. The mother stood behind the limb of the tree now lowering then raising the piñata, teasing the children to attract their interest.

They all knew how to play. The piñata had become standard at birthday parties, one of those items appropriated for its charm, yet offered to children without any explanation of its original uses. From party to party, all the children knew was that they must bat at it wildly in order to break it, so that they could scramble for its bounty.

The fat girl watched from a distance. She would not swim today, she did not feel like taking a turn at the piñata. She wandered into the playground and slumped into a swing, absent-mindedly kicking sand.

A blindfolded boy swung once at the piñata, hitting its side; the piñata spun around, and a few pieces of candy fluttered to the ground. The rest of the boys jumped on the candy in a huddle, knocking over the boy at bat.

"You said you knew how to play this game!" cried the mother, dropping the rope to help the fallen boy.

"The rules are that you wait to go for the candy until it *all* falls down," she insisted.

The boys looked surprised, and tittered "ahhh." They stood up and reformed their semicircle around the swinging donkey.

Another boy was blindfolded and handed the bat. He immediately swung at the piñata. The blow broke the donkey's leg, releasing another dribble of candy, and again the boys dropped quickly, as if by reflex to retrieve the sweets. Already they began to argue over the small Mars Bars, the miniature Sugar Daddies, the tiny Tootsie Rolls.

"Stop, stop this instant!" the mother shouted. The candy lay scattered like fallen fruit among the red plum leaves, the day cooling into late afternoon, the fog barely visible on the horizon.

"Well, we'll just have to open the donkey by hand and pull

out the rest of the candy and I'll distribute it equally. You just don't want to play this game right."

The children moaned a long "ohhhhhh" but did not complain further, did not ask to be taught how to play the game the way the mother wanted. Instead they quickly scattered, some onto the grass to wrestle, some toward the playground where the fat girl kept swinging and kicking sand.

The other girls reappeared fresh from the pool, wet hair close to their faces, beads of water dripping from their braids, giggling, towels slung across their thin shoulders. They moved like one body, in the direction of the swings.

In the distance, a chainsaw squealed through wet timber. A light breeeze, and more dry leaves settled on the grass.

"Okay all you kids!" the mother of the birthday boy shouted. "Pile onto the seesaw over there and let me take a picture."

The mother adjusted the lense of her camera, focusing on the empty seesaw.

"A picture?" shrieked the boys, as though she had asked to paint their nails or hug them.

The children shuffled toward the seesaw, kicking sand. The fat girl jumped off her swing to watch them, unsure of whether to join in. When they reached the chain-link gate they all tried to unhook the latch together.

"Boys against girls," said a soft voice from the center.

Another voice answered, "Yeah, Boys Against Girls. Boys Against Girls!"

The gate swung open, the boys quickly separated from the girls and jumped onto one end of the seesaw, positioning themselves as if for battle.

"Boys Against Girls, Boys Against Girls," they chanted. The girls climbed onto the opposite arm of the seesaw, joining in the refrain.

The seesaw teetered up and down as the children tried to balance themselves. "Boys Against Girls," they repeated in unison. Then the weight of the boys raised the girls high and higher. Half the chorus held the ground, half the air, as the light thinned and the fog began to roll in from the bay.

No Clubs Allowed

SOME GIRLS ARE VERY TOUGH. They're afraid of nothing. They're the ones who climb to the top of the jungle gym at school and jump, their hard bodies bouncing off the sand, their laughter crashing against the blacktop.

Two girls are jumping right now, hems flapping against the bars. It's good of course, girls so active, some mothers imagine athletic scholarships on the horizon, Stanford or Duke, whatever.

When the bell rings, Gabby goes down the street to an after-school program, glorified group babysitting. On a good day, arts and crafts, crocheted potholders, collages to pass the time, like patients in mental hospitals. Antoinette goes home on the bus. Runs up the three flights of stairs, gets to the top and goes down, goes up the stairs and down, again. Till Mama's home. Mama like mamas like papas has two bags of groceries in her arms for which she waited in two different lines at the supermarket and the vegetable market, after riding two buses to get to Auntie's in San Leandro. Antoinette flicks on a video game.

Early every evening she calls Gabby. She curls up on the couch. Gabby on her couch a couple of miles away. The two kids chat, a kind of parallel gossip, each furthering the conversation by a declaration, rather than a question.

"I'm upstairs," Gabby says. "Yes, when you come over, I've got toys in every room and my doggy's very happy."

"My birthday comes soon. I mean, you can come to my birthday party you know."

"Like, um, Sleeping Barbie is always sleeping. And, you know what? I gave Swimming Barbie a bubble bath. Her hair is silky and she dived right into the bubbles."

"My mama lets me have gum. And I chew it in the morning."

"My daddy takes me skating, and once he broke his leg."

"Are you happy?" a friend once teased Gabby.

"Of course," she shot back, at age four. "I've got a good life."

"You're micromanaging her life," my husband Don accuses me whenever I strain to arrange play dates for Gabby.

"You don't just walk down the street and find a friend," I shoot back. "This is corporate California."

I'm tired of cultivating for Gabby, and afraid if I stop, she won't have playmates from the public school we send her to. She'll only know her own narrow own. I promise myself to chill, as the teenagers advise, and let the children ask.

Antoinette's calls have become part of the day, like a meal. Gabby is happy after she hangs up, but it's her private happiness, and she doesn't talk about it.

I read to the girls at school, they're both bright, Antoinette already knows words, Gabby's on the cusp. Soon the world will split open for each of them, offering itself in sentences.

I watch the girls during recess. It's a cold day. The janitor distributes a box of naked Barbie dolls to the girls who don't want to do sports. Doll arms and legs are flung up on the ground near the sandbox. Antoinette is dressed like a doll, her hair tightly done up in braids with large colorful beads at the tips. They're jumping rope. Gabby chants *"and A my Name is Annie and I come from Alabama. . . ."*

"My Auntie come from Alabama," Antoinette says. "And my name begins with A and so does Auntie so I should use that, shouldn't I, when it's my turn!"

If we let Nature take its course here, nothing will happen outside school. I break my resolve and call Antoinette's mother. The call, I think, is a kind of small triumph, a piece of resistance against the terrible separateness of everything.

"The train is a-comin', oh yes, the train is a-comin', oh yes, Harriet Tubman, oh yes . . . Mama, we're not slaves!" Gabby announces. "Slavery is when people make you do things you don't want to do and don't say please and you have to take the underground railroad away and you don't have time to bake bread so you have to make flat bread and carry it on your back with little holes in it so it can breathe."

When I call Antoinette's mother, a man answers. Sleepy-voiced, he hands the phone over.

I introduce myself. Antoinette's mother pauses in a long silence that unnerves me. I'm direct and matter of fact by nature, weary from working, but experienced at calling strangers.

"Oh hello, uh-huh. Yes, I'm Anita."

"Oh, that would be nice. Dinner? Oh, I don't know."

"No she don't have no one to play with around here either."

More silence. I think, okay, how'll she get here? Bus too complicated, probably no car.

"Well, no, I don't, I don't have a car. But my boyfriend does."

"Well, that would be very nice, yes, I'm sure Antoinette would love it."

I write the address down in big letters so my husband can see it, get Gabby ready and head over to South Berkeley to get Antoinette. It's late afternoon. While I'm stopped at a red light, a street person taps on my window.

"What is it?" I moan.

"I want to ask you something," the street woman says. "Roll your window down, I want to ask you something."

I lean my elbow on the door lock and it goes click.

"What's the matter, lady? I'm not going to do anything to you, I just want to ask you something."

The light turns green and I drive off, upset.

When I pull up along Martin Luther King Jr. Way, Anita and Antoinette are waiting in front of a rundown apartment building.

A couple of men are walking out, and one stumbles behind a giant bottlebrush in full bloom. Then they both lean against the bars in front of low aluminum windows.

Anita stands beside Antoinette. Her long black add-on braids drape her shoulders. She is heavy, heavily made up, wearing bicycle shorts. Antoinette is delicate, freshly dressed for dinner.

We exchange a few words, and I promise to have the child home by eight.

I'm nervous, drive home nervously, make spaghetti nervously. I am distinctly aware of my house, which I rationalize is just a middle-class house. But I survey the furniture, the geometry of the rooms, the toys strewn everywhere, and try to cast a cold eye on the car outside, its value to others, what image it might give. I draw a blank; I am filled with dread.

The little girls play. Gabby is irritable about losing a game of checkers to Antoinette; Antoinette is older, more mature, says she knows how to ride a two-wheeler, rides it all over her neighborhood. Gabby can't. I wouldn't let her if she could. Won't let her walk alone to school around the corner. This time this world, no. I look at Antoinette fondly, glad she is smarter than my own child. Overjoyed she is not the one who is irritable, but the model guest.

Those men leaning against the dark bars, I think at dinner, their eyelids, their idle hands, those men do not define the homes inside, the child, her mother. This child, her sweet nature, slightly on the lookout, slightly on the edge of silence. Many no-teeth spaces in her mouth already, more than would have fallen out naturally at six, a silver cap, she says she once walked into a door. This child does not define her mother.

"If you squeeze your butt together," Antoinette says to Gabby, "it won't grow wide, you know."

The girls giggle, drop under the table.

"Who told you that, Antoinette?" Gabby asks.

"My auntie told me. She's a squeezer, you should see her."

Don slams the front door, heads for the mail. It's time to take Antoinette home. We all pile into his car, a black highly polished Saab, twelve years old, bought used. When we arrive at Antoinette's apartment building, we all get out. There are no lights at the entryway, a door buzzer hangs by its wires from the stuccoed wall.

We wait in front of the building, in front of the bottlebrush, its brilliant red flowers tickling our ears.

Don starts whistling "Some Enchanted Evening You Will Meet a Stranger," and the girls try to whistle with him.

Anita is halfway down the block, a grocery sack in her arms.

"Go round back," she tells the children, and I make introductions.

"Is that okay?" I say. "I mean, for them to be alone out back? There's no light."

"Oh they like to, Antoinette always likes to meet me at the door to the apartment."

My husband and I follow Anita up several flights of stairs. Our hands slide up the metal banisters. A sweet drug smell pervades the dark stairwell.

"You'll have to excuse the mess," Anita says, but when we enter the living room, it's very tidy. A sliding glass door looks out onto the Berkeley hills. The furniture is modern, neatly organized, shag carpeting. A television nests in a console case, next to pots of *diffenbachia* and wandering jew.

Anita sets down her grocery bag and immediately clicks on the TV. The children run into the bedroom, perch on the bed in front of dolls and stuffed animals neatly propped against the pillows, watch video games.

"She just loves those videos," Anita says. "Would you like something to drink?"

I see that Anita is twenty years younger than my husband and me. We are all self-conscious, Don laughs too loud, makes a remark Anita doesn't get but laughs at anyway.

"I love your view, gosh, the hills are twinkling."

"We just moved here from Napa in October, couldn't get Antoinette into a closer school," Anita says.

"Oh, it must be hard. I mean, how do you get her to school?"

"Well, we have to walk about six blocks to the bus. And then you know, there wasn't no after-school programs available 'round, here, I mean, none we could get into."

We chat for a few minutes, about the children. Anita wears sunglasses.

I round up Gabby and we all say our goodbyes.

On the drive home, Don and I begin to speak in our college Spanish, a convenient cover when we want to talk about Gabby in her presence.

"Speak my language," Gabby insists. "I don't like it when you don't speak my language."

"I don't want her going over to Antoinette's house," Don says. "*¿Comprende usted?* I mean, *¿Comprendes?* You want them to be friends, invite her to our house."

"*¿Por qué?*" I ask.

"*Porque* I don't like *los* video games, I don't want my child to sit in front of a TV and watch that *mierda.*"

"Well, it can't hurt every so often. What do you want? They can't play outside, obviously. *¡No pueden!*"

"Well, they can play outside if they play at our *casa.*"

"Well, I don't want her to go there because of that neighborhood. Look at that building. *¡Híjola!*"

"Yeah, another responsible landlord," Don says sarcastically.

Antoinette continues to telephone Gabby in the late afternoon. Then the phone calls stop, only no one notices.

"What happened to Antoinette?" I ask Gabby, weeks later, bending down to gather stray checkers under the table.

"She won't play with me anymore."

"What do you mean she won't play with you anymore? You were such good friends. Did you do something?"

"I didn't do anything."

"Did you say something?"

"No, we were on the playground, and she just stopped playing with me. Kanika and Makeesha came over and told her to stop playing with me."

"Stop playing with you? Why didn't you just play with them? Why didn't you just keep playing with Antoinette?"

"Well, Kanika and Makeesha have a club where Kanika charges members five dollars for overnights. And you know Mommy, the teacher said, 'no clubs allowed.' They're not supposed to have a club, there's no clubs allowed."

The business of the club. Impossible. What could this be about? I wondered. I'll ask the teacher, it's always good to talk to teachers, they have all the answers, don't they? Of course, there was no such thing. Not allowed. Glad you asked. Kanika's mom has been taking Makeesha and now Antoinette after school, and the teacher supposed the five dollars was what she charged the mothers.

"I wanna go to Kanika's, I wanna go to Kanika's," Gabby pleads when I explain the club business.

"You can't darling," I say. "You go to an after-school program near your house, and now they're going to a kind of after-school program near their house."

"You won't let me do anything, you never let me do anything!" Gabby yells.

"I have an idea, let's invite Antoinette to your birthday party. Is that great or what?"

Everything she does is so arranged, everything is so negotiated. We might as well be living in the suburbs, at least there she could ride a bike. Or New York, where it's everyplace all at once.

I send Antoinette and eleven other girls invitations to Gabby's birthday party. Gabby's birthday is the shining moment of the summer, and the preparations always take days. I bake and decorate the house and the porch with old-fashioned crepe paper and balloons, and arrange elaborate party favors for the children. There would be games, the sun would be warm, the day perfect as it almost always was.

Before I lick the stamp, I phone Antoinette's mother. I still have the address I wrote in block letters several months ago, tucked into the phone book among the other scraps of paper. But something warns me that the child might not live there anymore. After all, she had stopped calling. What rose up in me to imagine that? I dislike such thoughts, not the thought of the child's possible move, but the instability.

Anita answers, apologizes, she'd been napping, assures me yes, yes, she was still at the same address, and yes, she'd be able to bring her.

"What do she need?" Anita asks.

"I beg your pardon?"

"You know, for her birthday, like what size is she? What size dress do she wear?"

"Oh just, you know, there are so many of these parties, so many presents to buy, just a trinket, you know, don't go out of your way."

Gabby sits under a plum-tree bower all decorated with Chinese lanterns, at a small table by the side gate where the little girls enter the party. She's wearing a fancy party dress and a glittery crown that says Happy Birthday, greeting guests, giving each a princess crown and a wand. After fifteen minutes or so, all the children have arrived, and it's time for lunch of tuna sandwiches and potato chips and pink and yellow watermelon, pink lemonade.

"Where's Antoinette?" I ask Gabby, donning my own crown.

"Mommy, she's not here yet."

"Well, maybe she'll be here soon."

She is not there soon and she does not show up. I arrange the favors, slip a little brown ballerina in a pink tutu into each bag. As I light the birthday candles, I'm proud that the lemon cake turned out so perfectly, in spite of the dream that woke me at three in the morning. When I went to check it in the dream, one side of the cake had collapsed and chunked off, and ants and maggots were crawling in and out of holes they made as though my yellow cake was their personal hive.

Excited from the games and sweets, I think Gabby barely notices. About Antoinette not being there.

"Mommy, can we save a crown and the party favors for her, can we save the brown ballerina for Antoinette? Can we, Mommy?"

I bend down to pick up paper cups and napkins, and when I stand up, I'm dizzy. I look around the yard, into the neighbor's garden. These vines weighted with trumpet flowers, these treetops full of nests, these walkways animated by snapdragons, this beauty leaning in the direction of my gaze, this beauty does not define this place, which is partly mean and unbeautiful.

"Sure, honey, sure," I say sadly. "You can bring it to school in September."

Infant Sorrow

Struggling in my father's hands,
Striving against my swaddling bands,
Bound and weary I thought best
To sulk upon my mother's breast.
  —William Blake

IN THE CRYING, both of them going at it hard, neither child could say what happened. In between, a vague yet universal demi-language blurred by sobs, misunderstood.

You could hear them crying from down the block, down the hill, and they carried this weeping with them up the stairs, climbing slowly as though it weighed. They had left the house holding hands, they returned as echoes of each other. Against the distant horizon, two palm trees swayed away from them. That's how the wind blew that night, away from all of us, leaving the flora with frightened expressions.

The girls' faces were streaked with sooty tears, and each wheezed with any effort to speak. Mud streaked an elbow or two, knees were not without fresh scrapes.

Something always happens with young children to disturb

their equilibrium, and good parents, like firemen on duty, ready to slide down the pole in the firehouse, are on the alert even in their sleep. Awake, in the park, we had gone off duty for a little while, and we did not expect to be called up so soon.

We interrogated each child gently, so as not to disturb either's obvious suffering. We dimly remembered our early anguish through them, and we recognized in their suffering how our own parents wouldn't quite let us, wouldn't allow the frequent miseries of childhood to live out their natural course. How mother or father always implored us to cheer up, don't cry, it's not so bad. Or, the larcenous *We won't cry over that, will we?* forcing us into complicity with their adult restraint. Now we know we stopped crying then to be brave and to please them, and sometimes the crying seeped back inside and we didn't like to show any of it and we were secretly afraid of it in ourselves, even today. But we didn't want our children to be that way. We tried hard not to take their tears away from them. We didn't give them any advice about crying or tell them to stop doing it. We were of the mind that trying to stop a child from crying was like talking to the rain.

"So what happened?" we wanted to know. Of course, in order to speak, the girls would have to stop sobbing. And there is always some prideful inability to reverse the flow of tears just because it seems necessary. They'd been avowed best friends for months, and we hadn't seen this happen before, this sad, sudden anger between them. Surely we knew this could happen, did happen frequently with children, we could even recall it happening to us as children, but it was our first time as parents to witness our child's expressed love for another child turned to misery, yet still distinctly love.

"I hate her, I don't want to ever ever play with her again," was all our child would say. The definite quality of this assertion did not particularly faze us. We were certain it would pass.

"Tell us why?" we asked patiently.

But we were not really patient, we were annoyed that the outing had turned sour, that we were suddenly ousted as companions in pleasure. We had become, in a matter of moments, tall interlocutors.

There was no answer from either child, and a kind of smoky détente filled the air around them, as we sat in the waning light of late summer. The wind calm now, the palm fronds relaxed. "Did you hurt one another?" we asked foolishly. A long silence entered the room like a person, we adults glancing down at our nails, tossing off a glib remark about the weather that had nothing to do with the situation at hand.

The sobbing had ceased, a streak of sun parted the clouds, the wind picked up again. Something small darted across the roof, then the crunchy sound of dried leaves. One child nodded and the other turned away to stare out the window where the sky had turned pink and blue and fluffy like baby things.

We pointed in the direction of the stare. "Oh look children, look at that girl-and-boy sky!"

We who had been so careful with these sorts of designations could not resist. We could not resist the possible rise we might get out of one of the girls.

It was a trick, a trick of diversion and, we thought, of some elegance.

"We said mean things to each other," one child blurted out, almost penitently, but the other child didn't want to corroborate. She shut her mouth tight, turning down her small lips.

"What sorts of things?" we probed. The tone in our voice resembled tiptoes, if a tone could approximate, synesthetically, a movement. A slight pitch higher would move into unctuous patronizing.

The children wrinkled their noses and grimaced.

"Sweetie. . . ." we implored, our child staring right through us.

Frustrated, we began to press, oh so gingerly, to get to the bottom of it all. But there was no bottom and there was no easy getting. It would take as long as it needed. And the children knew that.

Minutes passed. Patience began its easy evaporation.

We could recall a slap across the cheek for the impertinence of silence, we could recall a few humiliating epithets admonishing us to listen, which of course required telling.

"Did one of you not listen to the other?" we brightened.

At last, one child nodded yes. Encouraged, we retreated, certain that our cautious forbearance would extract from each the exact words that might name and mend.

But we were no closer to the cause of the sorrow than when the children first trudged up the stairs. Now that the crying was officially replaced by sniffles, both girls snapped shut. We wanted to get it over with, to know what happened, to which child we might privately assign blame while holding each responsible to the other. But we could not yet satisfy ourselves by simply asking for apologies.

We wanted a story.

At last, when the pastel light left the sky, when dusk made us into silhouettes, we could no longer help ourselves. We burst out, "Did you?" And then, "Did she?" And after that, "Was there. . . ?"

Once we began the interrogation we could not stop, and we were rewarded with a steady, though measured flow of facts. Or were they innuendoes? It hardly mattered.

The narrative took shape, as though we knew all along what we expected them to tell us.

"She didn't want to do what I said!" one child shrieked.

"You you you . . . I hate you!"

"And you wanted her to stay?" we prodded, our patience running away from our reason. We marveled at how effortlessly we could reconstruct what we didn't witness.

"I wanted her to not run away. "
"You couldn't see her," we declared breathlessly.
The child nodded.
"And you got scared. . . ."
"And who hit who?" we ventured.
Neither would answer.
But both had fallen down, we were certain. The skinned knees, the dirty elbows. There must have been some pushing, shoving. . . .

So it had been like that. One child strayed from the other and the one left became frightened and angry. It all made sense now. This was cause for anguish.
At last, the sequence of the narrative in place, we were satisfied. We said we were sorry the two had fought and maybe they could play together some other time and not fight again, and one of us escorted the other child home.
"God, we work like serfs," we joked as we dropped into bed that night.

Days later, when the afternoon of the tears was past, when hundreds of small and large thoughts had circulated in our minds, and the occasion was assimilated in us like so many invisible molecules, our child made an announcement.
"In the park, you know what Susie said to me?"
"When, what?" we answered absently. We barely heard.
"She said she'd was going to throw me off the bridge. For real. And that made me cry."

A Little Window

the unlived, disdained, lost life, of which
one can die
            —Rilke

EVERYONE OWES NATURE a death. I know. My time is coming. I
wish I could send an understudy to pay my debt. But no sense
pushing it along by sitting still, no sense rushing toward a stop sign.

So I was mugged. So what. Nothing broke. I still got my health.
Who I really didn't want to read about it in the newspaper, who I
really didn't want to know that they took the envelope with the
money from the flea market, which of course, wasn't even mine, and
the keys, yes the keys, was my brother Harry. Christ! He always worried about me, when we were kids, it was always Harry interrogating
me, did I talk to the boy in the candy store, did I smile, did I tell him
where we lived? I'm alone now for eleven years, may he rest in
peace, Sam is gone, no children, and Harry says to me, "Adele, you
know there's no quota on robberies. Just because you were mugged
once, doesn't mean you're exempt. In fact, it's like money makes
money only in the negative. Adele," he begs me, "stay home!"

Stay home! What, I ask you, am I supposed to do at home? Who am I supposed to talk to? You want me to stay home and wait to be taken to heaven? You want me to stay home and die of boredom?

Yes, I know, I know what that Pascal said, about ninety-nine percent of all man's problems start when he leaves his room. This could be true for a man, but frankly, for a woman, it's the reverse.

When I leave my room, my life begins. Finally. At last. Yes. I'm not saying I didn't live, that Sam and I didn't live, it's not true. We traveled, we ate, we drank, we worked. Certainly we loved. But to live with a man is to live through him, just as to live with a woman is the same. It's a screen, it's a protection, it's a good thing to hold hands in a dark movie. But when a good thing is over, a person might not want another good thing, you know? A person might just want a new thing,

Harry doesn't understand these issues. He's what they call a nurturing man. This is what I heard a top psychologist call such men, always concerning themselves with the welfare of others close to them. Harry does the same thing to Estelle, his wife. He calls her five times a day, sometimes just to ask her how to spell a word. He grabs onto her arm when they cross the street! But you know, it's a fine line between concerning and smothering. Will you get a load of that word I just used, smothering? Just tack on a little *s* and you've got a monster!

There are worse things in the world, I admit. People are starving, and the CEO of Hewlett Packard is making $15,000 a day! What kind of man is he? You, my sweet young friend, may not enjoy the social security benefits I enjoy. The newspaper is offering new obscenities every morning.

Headlines, oh yes, headlines, Woman Dies of Boredom. Diagnosis confirmed, prognosis foreseen. Harry would like it if I locked myself away, he says to me, "Adele, you go downtown with all those fake rings and bracelets, you think a thief is going to look at you with a magnifying glass to see if they're real? All he sees," and Harry claps his hands here, here is where Harry gets dramatic, "all he sees," and of course Harry was like this when we were kids, pausing, timing, so you waited for the punch line, but it was never as good as the pause, oh, it reminds me of sex, sex with Sam, it was never, you should excuse me Sam, as good as the idea of sex with Sam, not that I'm an expert, or like I've had so much other sex I could tell you what, but I remember thinking about Sam and what he'd do and how, at least in the beginning, the thought was *sexy!*

So Harry claps his hands together, and this is very Jewish, even if he doesn't say, *Oy Gevult*, it sounds like it, in between the lines, and the gesture he makes, well, we're second generation, so we're acculturated, the gesture is the vestige, the Jewish shadow, in that pause of Harry's. The shadow of shtetl fear.

"All he sees," says Harry finally, "this thief, this *gonnif*, is that you, old lady, are bejewelled!

"You are a fat, crippled, old lady with jewels! He knocks down your cane and *voilà!* He's got you."

To argue with Harry is to fight a force of nature, a force only a year older than me but knock on wood, still ferocious.

So Harry would like me, because I got bad arthritis, to stay in, but No Way José.

Once, I was watching a play, a matinée, and it was over, and I was laughing and crying and clapping, and a woman next to me, she leans over, and says, "So, what did you think of the ending?"

"Well, I say," and I catch myself, she looks gentile, she's a stranger, you gotta show some restraint. "Well . . . Who are you?" I say.

"I'm the playwright," she says.

I clap my hands. "Gimme your autograph please!" And she does and I tell her I love the ending, except, it ties things up together a little, like a drawstring bag. I tell her, make a little window, open it up a little, you could open it up, and let us, the Active Audience, make up our own minds.

You be the judge. If I listened to Harry, I wouldn't have gotten mugged, the envelope wouldn't have disappeared, the keys wouldn't be floating around the city from pocket to pocket to garbage can, useless like a bunch of lost teeth. But who cares about lost teeth? You lose a tooth at my age you go to the dentist and have a shiny new fake one made. Of course, I wouldn't stay home if I was on my last leg, I mean, my last, and I still got two.

Loosestrife

WE'D BEEN HAVING some trouble with the neighbors again.

"Thank God for marital strife," my husband laughed as he leaned out the window with a beer in his hand.

Against the advice of a clerk at the East Bay Nursery, I was out back planting more *lythrum salicaria* this year. Purple Loosestrife, a hardy perennial herb, the tag said.

"A bitch to start, but then invasive, and that means if it takes, you'll never get rid of it unless it dies in a frost," the nurseryman moaned.

It seems the couple next door got into a bad fight and the next day the wife packed up the kids, took the good car, and drove off.

"I slapped her around a little, but she'll come to her senses," her husband said confidently to my husband. "She's a Christian woman."

As though being a Christian, going to church on Sunday, and singing hymns absolves anyone. Now, I have no particular regard for the woman next door who left her husband. In fact, I hate her because of how she talked to her kids when her husband wasn't around.

"What is your problem?" she screamed at the littlest one after he'd fallen off his tricycle and been crying for twenty minutes.

But I was rooting for her not returning on several counts.

There appears to be a limited number of slots available in the world for happy marriages. From the day this now unhappy family moved in next door, my husband and I fought. We fought over the noise in the neighborhood and we fought especially about the noise next door. We have irreconcilable differences about noise. He thinks it will never go away and thus we should ignore it. And I think ignoring is related to ignorance and you can't get ignorant again.

It's always been a turbulent block, but there were a few years of calm after our original neighbors abandoned the ill-fated house.

I was out of town when my husband called me with the news: "There's a pickup outside and they're loading it up with the furniture."

"Ours?" I laughed.

"No, it seems that Earl and Marilyn had a big fight over Earl's drinking, he slapped her around a bit, and she's moving out with the kids."

This family had a set of mean teenagers and bad taste in music. I was thrilled when they split up. But skeptical.

Would we at last enjoy a little privacy on account of someone else's conjugal misery? Would the sound of the wind in the weeds next door lull us to sleep instead of Earl's nightly rendition of *I've been loving you for a long time, I ain't gonna stop nowww,* followed by Marilyn mincing no words on him for not mowing the lawn?

Who would have imagined that we wouldn't even mind it too much when a piece of their roof crashed down into our shared driveway during the last heavy rains, eaves and all, bird's nest, eggshells, tiny yolks.

No one could have predicted how long this house would lay fallow.

Ordinarily you think of women gossiping, but in my neighborhood, the men stand around in gangs of four or five drinking beer and yakking while one of them sweats over a carburetor or fiddles with the starter on an ancient power mower. Sometimes they hang out on somebody's front porch, cooing and babbling so you can't really hear until them until a big *hee-haw* bounces off the concrete. They all know which teenage girl is going out with who, whose mama said she couldn't, why the twins across the street lost their scholarship to that school too far from home.

They also know other things that happen on the block, things they don't tell their wives until they've figured out a way to soften the disclosure.

"You know that crazy guy?" my husband said to me casually one day. "The one who hops around the street in his socks and lives in the shed with all those computer parts and pipe wrenches? Well, the other day he dragged an old couch onto the lawn and doused it with kerosene."

"And then what, dear?"

We're bookended by the behaviorally different. There's a high proportion of nut cases roaming the streets, especially since former Governor Ronald Reagan shoved them out of the nut house twenty years ago and gave them one-way bus tickets to Berkeley. But nowadays there are more varieties of insanity. Every day thousands of people are driven crazy by the lack of a bed, a roof, and a steady diet.

They rattle around as though the bottles and cans clanking against the metal mesh of their shopping carts played the terrible music of their personal despair. It's easier to maneuver a cart right down the middle of the street. You don't have to push and drag it over sidewalks swollen from rebellious tree roots, across driveways, around toys, past malicious dogs.

When Earl and Marilyn broke up, everyone on the block started to speculate over what would become of the place as it deteriorated, and they didn't mind asking us. Neighbors stood around shaking their heads. After the big earthquake, everyone had an opinion about the structural damage. "Why, they couldn't get more than two spits in a bucket if they put this doghouse on the market," one neighbor said.

"Boy, I'd offer them a few thousand in cash and knock it down," another countered.

Men and women who had rarely hammered a nail in the wall enthusiastically provided estimates of what it would take to repair the kitchen floor that was rumored to have rotted away.

By the time the front porch collapsed, roof rats were running in and out of the basement, and wild buckwheat blossomed in the yard. People remarked how profligate the owners were not to rent it out or sell it, with the housing shortage and all.

We could not afford to buy the house, we did not care to go to prison for burning the house down, we did not want to encourage the owners to care for the house. And we could not offer the house to those who might need it.

I was amazed that homeless people weren't drawn to the place.

Then one morning, a woman with several front teeth missing rang my doorbell.

"Eh, hello, I'm wondering," she said, "if I could sweep your porch, or, ah, the front of your house for some money. I need seventy-five cents or so to get home."

Stunned, I asked her if she had a broom.

"No," she smiled. "I'm not no professional or nothing. I just need to get some money together to get home."

"Okay," I said. "Meet me 'round back, I'll get you a broom."

She swept and she swept. Back inside, time warped, like it had turned into the thirties and she had come to my quiet little farmhouse looking for honest work after the sheriff ran her out of town for the crime of vagrancy.

But it's the nineties. She's sweeping up leaves mixed with candy wrappers and broken whiskey bottles discarded by patrons of the liquor store across the street.

"Where you headed?" I intruded, as she bent down to shove the debris into the dust pan.

"Oh 14th and Broadway. I was on my way to visit my grandmother, but . . ." and I drifted as she described her setback, too caught in my own thoughts. How could her grandmother live at 14th and Broadway? There are nothing but office buildings on 14th and Broadway in downtown Oakland, and most of the single-room-occupancy hotels nearby have been condemned by the city or demolished.

"Would you happen to have any other areas for me to sweep? I could use the work," she said.

I glanced over at the driveway, the scattered dry rot from the fallen eaves next door.

"Sure," I pointed to a pile of moldy shingles and offered, with a perverse generosity, that the house next door was abandoned. I was hoping she'd take the hint. "Just ring my bell when you think you've finished."

Inside I scanned a newspaper story on Russian housewives forced to sell their bodies through escort services because wages had dropped so low after the breakup of the Soviet Union. A twelve-year-old girl picked up for prostitution said she needed money to buy a Barbie doll. I watched the homeless woman through the slats of my living room blinds. Her face looked old enough to be my mother's; her tiny body, bending to pick up a soggy carton, disappeared beneath an oversized sweatshirt with a Calvin Klein logo.

Fifteen minutes later she rang and handed me the broom. I glanced at the driveway, perfectly swept down to the oil stains.

"How much do you want for your labor?" I asked.

"A couple of bucks will do it," she smiled. Face to face again, I could see that she wasn't old, just worn.

When I handed her a ten, she thanked me profusely.

"God will surely bless you even if I can't," she said and walked down the street to the bus stop.

Occasionally, over the next few years, the owners of the house next door would stop by. Most people wouldn't notice that they'd been there. The husband or the wife, but never together, would open the padlock on the basement door and drag out a piece of furniture, shove it into a pickup, and drive off. Once an older woman in a shiny car drove up, stared at the string of broken Christmas lights dangling from the porch, and drove off. Weekly, the Jehovah's Witnesses trudged up what was left of the front steps and bang-bang-banged on the front door. Their plaintive hellos resounded across the vacant driveway.

One morning I looked out into the high weeds next door and discovered that they were parted by two colorful bedrolls. As though instinctively aware of my glare, a figure emerged, stretched itself in the early sunlight, a lovely dark Venus-on-the-half-shell sort of girl. Her handsome companion leapt out of his sleeping bag and the two kissed. From the quality of their movements, they were probably no more than teenagers. I watched them make their morning toilet, splash water from a canteen on their faces, shake their dreadlocked hair, and pack up their gear.

Wouldn't you like to live here? I beckoned them psychically.

In a moment they disappeared.

The house next door repelled even the transient.

Last fall, after years of relative hush, a large van from the ShotGun Delivery Service pulled up and blocked our shared driveway, and a couple of burly men began dragging a paisley couch up the steps. They were followed by a diminutive dog, the kind with jaws that were too small to retrieve the morning paper.

The name of the company inscribed on this truck bothered me more than it ought to. There had recently been a series of armed robberies in the area, assisted by Uzis.

Cousins were moving in. Not mine. The owner's. The house next door was about to be teeming with new tenants.

You must understand, these houses are so close, if the shades are up, you can see the corn on the cob the people are having for dinner. You can see the husband clipping his nose hair in the bathroom mirror, you can see the pilot light flickering in the space heater that nests in the false hearth. Worse, you can hear more than is decent to hear, such as,

"Why didn't you go to church with me this morning?" the wife queried the husband in the living room, after several hours of tense silence, followed by screen-door slamming, huffing and puffing and frenetic busyness in the backyard.

"Well, I was gonna," he replied meekly. No matter that he'd began working on the first of many six-packs just before his wife left for church at 9 a.m.

"No, don't you lie to me, you was not gonna, you just sat around and drank."

"I meant to go to church today, I really did." He pulled another can of beer off the plastic-ring holder. "But God, the pressure, it's, I can't take it no more."

The husband was working at least six days a week and long hours. Every morning between six-thirty and seven-thirty he would slam the front door after a conversation with one of the kids and drive off in the ShotGun van to make deliveries all day. And then there was the pressure the wife must have felt with all those children, one or two still swaggering around in diapers. . . .

The husband spotted the youngest racing into the room and grabbed him by the arm. "What you still doing with that bottle, boy? That's it! Gimme that! No more!"

He ripped the bottle out of the child's grip and the rest of the scene was tears-tears-tears, until the little boy flung himself down on the floor and kicked up a good fit.

The wife marched out the back door, followed by a howling golden retriever and a yapping Pomeranian that was destined to be tied to the garage door for the day.

I was in the garden, checking on the sages and the loosestrife, which wasn't doing very well. Apparently, it hadn't taken root yet, but gardening requires belief in the unseen.

All of the activity next door complemented the sirens wailing in the immediate distance. The hippies down the block struck up an impromptu bluegrass rehearsal. Several revving motorcycles in the liquor store parking lot, low-flying jets, and a chorus of chain saws heralded autumn home-improvement projects across the street.

Children zoomed up and down the cement driveway in Hot Wheels and plastic kiddie cars clackety-clacking. One of the neighborhood nuts walked by, stopped abruptly, and pulled up his shirt. He began scratching his belly, rubbing it in small concentric movements around his navel, then all over his middle, laughing hysterically.

"Breathe these voices!" he screamed.

Spring came, and then summer ascended. The *lythrum* didn't bloom. No purple spiked ovoids like the nursery tag said. Not even any new branches.

I was ready to move out or have my hearing disconnected or blocked like those people who have their stomachs surgically stitched so they won't eat so much. After all, I knew a tarot reader on Telegraph Avenue who poked out his eyes for visionary purposes. I contemplated a silent world, even though I read in the newspaper that John Cage said there was no such thing as silence.

But suddenly the next-door neighbors broke up. First the wife disappeared with the kids. And then a few weeks later, in the middle of the night, another woman dragged the abandoned husband across the lawn and into the ShotGun van. A cloud of exhaust from a broken tailpipe, and they were gone. An old-fashioned cardboard suitcase quietly leaned against the trash cans under the back steps and kept on leaning there.

Luck isn't a lady, it's a break, a wave of action you can't control, something bigger and better than you, better maybe than God.

The days turned quiet and warm, the nights were quiet and warm, and the shades next door were drawn. Pink dahlias the size of basketballs began to bloom along the driveway right under our bedroom windows, but I don't think anyone ever planted them, certainly not me.

The Dean's Widow

SHE WAS OLD and she was a widow, the widow of the dean. Once, a dean used to be some kind of general in the ranks of the academy. So that when a dean was dead and when you had been a professor's wife, a professor who had worked for thirty-five years under the umbrella of this dean, and when this dead dean had once lived up the street from you, well, he is still dean.

The life he leaves behind is the life of a dean. And the woman he leaves behind is the widow of the dean, living the life of the dean and his wife, only something's missing.

The widow of the dean needs sex, she announced to the widow of the biology professor.

"Humpf," the widow of the dean grumbled. "I need to go to bed with a man and so do you, Penny," Miranda commanded, biting into a buttercream from a Whitman's Sampler.

Whitman's Sampler, she said to herself. How did my life come to this?

"This chocolate is so so gooey," the widow of the dean said, coughing.

"Yes you do," said Penny, the widow of the professor, out of habitual deference. "I suppose you do need it, Miranda, but of course, I'm past that, I don't really think of myself as anyone who...."

"Well that's your problem, Penny, it's always been your problem," the widow of the dean said. "You don't think of yourself at all."

If Penny disagreed with the dean's widow, she did not say.

Miranda lit another cigarette, took a long drag, and stuck out her well-manicured nails, bright crimson flicking past Penny's peripheral vision like a red-winged blackbird.

The widow of the dean was expecting a guest next week. A gentleman caller, so to speak. A house guest. Old beau from college, a widower. Dentist from Georgia. They had kept in touch over the years, a few visits, Christmas cards with photos, newsy annual letters his wife wrote.

"Don't patronize me, Penny, take me shopping. I need some new lingerie before he comes."

She tapped her red fingernails on the metal of her cane, click-click-click.

"Well, I've got a Victoria's Secret catalogue?" Penny said, as she always did, with a kind of question mark and rise at the end of any assertion she made. "I keep trying to get off their mailing list. But they insist. I even wrote them an unpleasant note to remove my name forever. You'd think they're trying to tell me something?"

"Look here," she looked through the bottom half of her glasses, licking her index finger before she turned the page. "*Our Exclusive private sale issue brings you a great collection of tempting buys, wardrobe updates and fabulous basics. . . .*"

"Wardrobe update!" screeched the widow of the dean. "Nothing wrong with my damn wardrobe!"

"But look, it says, *Save $10 on the iced pink chemise. Lit with sequins, the empire bodice has a tiny covered button and organza lining; satin charmeuse falls softly to the hem. Slim, adjustable straps. Imported poly.*"

"Or this," she pointed. "This is beautiful, Miranda. *Save $20 on our sinus,* I mean, *sinuous, full-length gown on a reverse jacquard of satin with a sheer floral pattern; beautifully shaped with princess seams and a high side slit. Pale pink or white.*"

"What did you say?" said Miranda. "High side what?"

"High side slit, Miranda," Penny repeated carefully.

Miranda often needed a bit of help getting over to Penny's. Recently, Penny had her walkway widened so that her friends could get to her door more graciously. Penny lived just down the block but she worried about Miranda's going a little blind and a little deaf.

For the past several years, Miranda had become more difficult in proportion to her age. Her social life had been dwindling to faculty women's luncheons and memorial services—old friends from administration on to the Great Divide, the president of the university gone, and no one to flirt with.

I'm a living time bomb, Miranda thought. So I might as well get off while I can.

"I'm a living time bomb," she said to Penny, after they'd placed the rush telephone order to Victoria's Secret.

Miranda insisted on next-day delivery.

"Now Miranda," Penny always tried to soothe her. "Now, dear."

"Don't. . . ."

"Well Miranda, why don't we just think of him as your romance, your possible . . . romance?"

"OK," Miranda said, lighting up another cigarette. "You can think of it any way you like. But where there's smoke," she said coughing, "I'm out to make fire."

Miranda was out to catch a man. Not just any man. A man with the kind of character and stature and power afforded her by her former husband, gone now a decade, her dearly beloved not recently deceased husband.

In the lives of the old, ten years is a short time. But in the lives of the unloved, ten years is an eternity.

I'm tired of this purgatory, Miranda thought.

"I'm tired of this purgatory," she said.

After the last bridge club meeting, Miranda added an entry to her memoirs: *I had no one to talk to but faculty wives. Wives wives wives, nothing left but sexless wives who were still trapped in the kitchen. Well-meaning but unsophisticated women who sacrificed everything, even eros, for devotion. It never occurred to them to be otherwise. They were left over from an era when a young Ph.D. chose a mate like a footstool for its upholstery, the deep pile that might cushion his brittle, clawing ascent toward full professorship. But the men of my time were charged with ideas, and ideas held for me a profound eroticism. I had nothing in common with these women and could not hide my contempt for their deference to their husbands. When the men died, one by one, their talk died with them. But I was alive with desire. What was I to do with this longing?*

"Penny," she said. "Do you think women look sexier with their hair tied back or their hair loose?"

"Well, Miranda, I don't know."

"Penny, the reason you don't know is because your hair is so damned short that you've forgotten. Why is it that older women cut their hair so damned short and why is it that they come out of beauty parlors stinking of chemicals and looking like poodles?"

"I don't know, Miranda. What were you thinking? Oh Miranda, are you thinking of dyeing your hair? Oh it would look so pretty . . . a soft auburn, something not too dark, but so that it wouldn't clash with your new iced-pink chemise. . . ."

"Where's your beauty parlor, Penny?"

"Oh, Miranda, I hate to tell you. I've been going there forever. You know how loyal I am. But now it's, it's in the War Zone."

"You mean over there by the base? No thanks. You want to hasten my demise, you want me to be the first victim of a drive-by shooting on her way to get her hair done? What a headline. Widow of the Dean Shot Before a Touch-Up. Penny, do you have any idea what's going to happen when that military base closes? The war will escalate. You better find yourself another hairdresser, *tout de suite*."

Penny, widow of the professor, the biology professor, had a thought or two about the widow of the dean's recent ideas.

What is she thinking? thought Penny. She's ready to sell everything and go off with a man she hasn't seen in years. It's preposterous that Miranda should even imagine it. What's making her so sexy? It can't be sex, can it?

I haven't touched a man since the dean died, thought Miranda. If I don't touch a man before I die, I'm going to die without touching another man! Christ!

"*Fried Green Tomatoes* is on at eight, Miranda. It was such a wonderful book. It's about friendship."

Sometimes Penny had a way of not asking but offering, and this got on Miranda's nerves. Penny had once worked for a man who insisted that she never ask him a question. He instructed her: "If you want me to do something, just say, The letter needs your signature, sir. Never, I mean never, say, Would you please sign the letter, sir?"

Oh no, thought Miranda, this movie is going to be like her Duncan Hines/Cherry Pie Mix cakes.

"Oh dear," said Penny, several times during sad scenes.

"Christ," said Miranda. "I hate crying involuntarily during movies."

"Oh, the bastards!" Penny said, when the KKK began lashing the black man, his back oozing miserably, his face rigid.

"I'm tired," sighed Miranda. "Why don't I just go on home?"

"Oh Miranda, wait a little bit, it's almost over, then I'll walk you."

Miranda shut her eyes, thinking, oh boy, when it's over, I'll get to hear the height of her critique. Well Done, she'll say. Or, Nicely Handled. I have got to leave this town.

Miranda drifted off, thinking of sex with the dentist from Georgia, thinking of Georgia, peaches, plantations, summers on Hilton Head, etc.

"Well done!" shouted Penny a little while later. Miranda sat straight up.

Bainbridge, the dentist from Georgia, arrived with a small leather suitcase and an undetermined internal disorder that necessitated his staying with Miranda for five days and going to the university hospital for tests.

He arrived in a taxi, did not rent a car because he could not drive on account of cataracts.

"How fortunate for us that there were no specialists who could diagnose you properly in all of Georgia," Miranda said to the dentist, charmingly, over tea and reminiscences. The years had left him handsome.

"You look well, Bainy," she smiled. "You were always so distinguished."

"Why, thank you, Miranda dear," he smiled.

"I do hope you'll be comfortable in the guest room, dear."

"Oh Penny," she said later, holding the bedroom phone close. "Oh, he's here, he's here. Bainbridge is here. Bainy, I called him in college. You know, I've always always cared for him, in spite of the fact, that of course, I did love the dean tremendously, but it was an altogether different affection, and as we know, each of us is so various, we can love many in a lifetime. In fact, I don't believe I've even been unfaithful to him, by marrying the dean, because, it wasn't the same kind of love that I was giving or getting. Did you know I slept with men before I married the dean?"

"Oh Miranda," Penny sighed, who had loved and tolerated only the biology professor. "Take it slowly, will you?"

"Oh Penny, I'm in the biggest of hurries. I'm going to put on that pink chemise tonight, after dinner."

The following afternoon, Bainbridge Bellows, DDS, accepted the margarita that Miranda fixed for him after his morning of tests. They toasted for old times' sake. He was an exceptionally quiet man whose broad smiles showed off his impeccable dentures.

"Why don't we," Miranda suggested after the second margarita, "oh why don't we fill the thermos with the rest of these drinks and take a taxi to the lake?"

The dentist smiled and said he thought that a splendid idea.

They drank and laughed and Miranda told stories about her travels, her dead pet African Grey. She evaluated a new novel by a brilliant Japanese Englishman that Penny's daughter-in-law had recommended to their book club. She offered analysis of the economic decline of the middle classes. They leaned on each other's arms and walked up the path to Penny's house and had more drinks and dinner there and soon it was time to go home.

Five days passed very slowly. The dentist, though friendly and ready to listen, exhibited a reserved nature. He made no particular requests, phoned no other friends, and shut his door at night. In the morning, he would ask Miranda how she slept. She would tell him in great detail, even recount her dreams, and he would say nothing in return. A routine set in, punctuated by his morning visits to the hospital. In the afternoons, he would read, flip through magazines, turn the television on and off and on again, watch tennis matches, golf. Miranda would try to engage him in talk, make dinner plans, tire herself, retire to her bedroom alone, and phone Penny.

"Why don't you join us for a special dinner at that fancy new Le Paraggi?" asked Miranda.

Of course, as Miranda's oldest and dearest friend, Penny said she wouldn't think of not driving them.

"Bainbridge, why don't you sit in the front seat where you can see the sights better, dear?" Miranda said.

The softly lit decor of the restaurant featured a bevy of young handsome Italian waiters and waitresses, all with romantic accents, apparently imported just to work there.

"*Buona sera*, table for three?" said a young Sophia Loren stand-in.

"My goodness," said Penny. "I didn't know there were so many recent I-talian immigrants in this town."

"Let's have a bottle of this lovely chianti," Miranda said. "Won't that be right, Bainbridge? Do you remember all the chianti we drank in college?"

Bainbridge said he did, as he gazed at the menu.

"Well, I've heard the veal is very good. And look, they have *bruschetta*. I love *bruschetta*. Don't you, Bainbridge?"

The beautiful waitress leaned into the perfect isosceles triangle created by the heads of the three diners.

"And we have a be-u-ti-fal, *molto bello, zuppa di escarole e riso*, with fresha sauteed escarole, or if you prefer, a very light *zuppa di* yellow esquash and blossoms, an especial *cacciatora de mare* with lobster, crab, and prawn and fresh fennel Pernod saffron sauce, a calamari lightly estuffed weetha green chile cornbread and fresha wild *funghi*, oh that ees mushrooms, and how do you say, oh, yes, braysed een white wine and dark beer. I will leeve you to think on it."

"For *i primi*," Miranda said, "I'm going to have the *gnocci con funghi*. Or maybe this polenta with goat cheese and whole baked garlic and peasant bread sounds interesting. What will you have, Bainy?"

"Oh," he said as he surveyed the menu. "Oh I don't know. Whatever you think is best, Miranda."

On the sixth day, after a light lunch, Bainbridge Bellows phoned for a taxi, thanked Miranda for her hospitality, promised to write, and left for the airport.

"He must be very sick," Miranda later said to Penny on the phone.

"What is it?"

"He wouldn't say."

"And?"

"Oh, we liked one another, but it's exactly the way it was fifty years ago."

"How could that be, Miranda? How could it be the same?"

"Oh," she sighed. "He's incredibly dull."

"He didn't feel like having any, uh, sex?" Penny said.

"No," Miranda said. "No, he didn't feel like it."

Man

A CERTAIN MAN I KNOW is brought to tears by the misfortunes of others. He weeps hardest for innocent civilians in faraway places slaughtered by oppressive regimes, or ideals that have fallen suddenly like crashed statuary. Next, he weeps hard for the miseries of acquaintances—cancer, car accidents, paralysis, etc. On several occasions, he has phoned me with the tearful news of the death of a childhood friend he has not seen in thirty years or the plight of a friend of his great uncle who was forced into destitution or held up at gunpoint and badly beaten. I have known him to empty his pockets at the sight of a homeless family on the sidewalk. He never weeps over his own misfortunes, though he will rush back to a restaurant if he suddenly recalls that he has not left the waitress enough tip. This man is rarely brought to tears by the exacting and terrible things that happen to those he is closest to. It is not for lack of terrible things in the lives of those he loves and sees daily. Many untoward and even devastating things have happened to him and to his next of kin—diseases, injustices, injuries, loss. Yet he does not weep for them. Whenever anyone close to him tells him a sad story or recounts an emotion, he leaps up to get something in the kitchen or remembers a phone call he failed to return. He cannot concentrate on sentences long enough to read more than a few each day. He cannot not fix something broken or assemble something new without getting up every few minutes to do something else, and soon the activity is left unfinished. He has to force himself to end anything. After a lifetime of interruptions, jerk starts, good intentions, he falls asleep but is awakened by a fear of his own dream. Sometimes he channel surfs until dawn. He cannot sit without tapping his foot or clipping his nails, he cannot eat dinner without pouring glass after glass of wine, or water. If the telephone rings, he flies to answer it, no matter that his wife has just revealed suicidal thoughts. This man owns multiple versions of gadgets, coffee pots, tools, etc., because, like a squirrel with his walnuts, he forgets where he put what he's bought. However, should he encounter a dead squirrel on the lawn or a mouse caught in a trap, he will burst into inconsolable tears.

Nothing Compared to

MONA'S A PLUMP, SWEET twin who cuts my hair and writes poetry. She's got an edge to her humor but she's compassionate, and you can tell she was brought up well. She bought my books long before she started cutting my hair, and as a very insecure person about things like haircuts, I felt welcomed by the thought that she knew my work. Mona's never shown me a poem of hers, but sometimes she'll tell me when she's gone to an open-mike reading at some pizza place near campus or some punk club in the Mission.

Her twin sister Donna, who has an abrasive, unsweet temper, recently took up poetry too after years of acting. They were close when Mona first started cutting my hair, but now they don't talk. Mona says Donna has an identity problem and ought to get a life.

"It's painful for me to talk about," Mona says, "but how could she call herself a poet? She couldn't write her way out of dime bag."

Every part of the perimeter of both Mona's ears is pierced, with tasteful tiny gold or silver hoops. The soft eyebrow area above one eye also has a pierce, and of course one nostril has a very discreet sparkly stud. Recently, during my last haircut, I noticed she had pierced the center of her chin—a bright brassy stud, more like a tack, glinted in the sunlight as she reached for a hand mirror and another pair of scissors.

We were talking hair, of course. It's amazing how much there is to say about it. It just doesn't compare to anything, and it's such an illusion, we both agree. Mona thinks of herself as a hair artist. You'd think, as two poets, we'd talk more about poetry, but Mona doesn't read much. The spoken word is her genre.

She had decided to let her color fade, and go Punk Earth Mama Natural. Which for her, she explained, was an ashy blond but how would she know since she'd been dyeing her hair for half her life? "Ash Tray Blond," she laughed, though that was hard to imagine from the warm burgundy shade she'd been since I'd known her. The color of her hair seemed to be the color of her, a sensitive person, with eyebrows and lashes dyed to match.

"Well," she said, cutting the back of my hair. "I'm going completely natural. No more dye. No more drugs or alcohol, you know, for two years now. So no more hair color."

I suspected a planned pregnancy in the making. Women these days seem to get very natural right before or just after they've conceived. This state of mind precedes the search for wooden toys. The desire for purity, as a starting place, as if that place were the true nest.

She confirmed, with a soft "Who Knows?" The kind of Who Knows that's reserved for babies in the making. *First* babies, usually.

Mona will be the third hair artist I've lost to babies.

"Yes," she ran her fingers through her very short red hair. "I'll be Natural. And look," she said paratactically, as she rolled up the sleeve of her black T-shirt. "I got a tattoo."

As if tattoos were the most natural things known to woman, in fact, the pinnacle of *au naturel*.

A face-like five-or-six-inch design sat squarely on her bicep. Blue curly flourishes, that dark denim tattoo blue, surrounding several red points for eyes, tribal-like, a couple of yellow dots randomly dotting the perimeter. A gargoyle-like affair.

"Oh, isn't it beautiful?" she asked. "I want to get another one right above it."

"It's amazing," I said. I couldn't think of anything else to say, except, "What's the next one going to be?" But as with children's drawings, you're not supposed to say, What's that? You're supposed to point and query, Tell me about it, according to mental health professionals.

She pointed to the spot where in myself and others I know, bursitis or arthritis or what the Chinese lovingly call "fifty-year-old shoulder," already staked a claim like a sign advertising the site of a new suburban business park.

"Yeah," she said, "right here."

"So tell me," I said, as she cut my bangs on an angle, "tell me about the pain."

"Well, it was only an hour and a half. I mean that's not long."

Tiny hairs fluttered past my eyelashes onto the tiled floor.

"But did it hurt?" I pressed, asking the same thing everyone else must have asked for the last week.

People who get tattoos like to show them, so they have to expect questions about pain, don't they?

"Well," she said. "I've had menstrual cramps that were worse. I mean, that's inside you and this, why this pain is only on the surface."

I nodded, in complete agreement, as if I knew.

"It was nothing, I mean nothing," she said, "compared to getting a nipple pierce."

She handed me the hand mirror so I could admire how she'd sculpted the back of my hair. Nothing radical but shorter at the nape than the sides. Very stylish. I swiveled myself around in the chair and held the mirror up to the mirror so I could see her perfectly straight face in it.

Columbus Day

"SHUT UP, JUST SHUT UP!" he snarls at the silent passengers across the aisle.

Dark greasy hair stuck to a skull. Sweaty temples. Glassy, colorless eyes that seem to penetrate but don't quite follow through on their gaze, darting from person to person like small voracious birds among berries. Fringes on a rawhide vest in constant animation. Kicks the aisles with ripped toes, soles flap up like two dumb tongues.

The parts of a human rise and stench rises, is the body of a man, a trembling disintegration leaning against the doors of the commuter train. Above, a warning sign imploring passengers not to lean against the doors.

"Shut up!" he screams louder and flips his middle finger up to anyone.

The clean-shaven men, fragrant young women do not respond, glance, turn away, defer mutely to this troubling presence. Tourists stare, then resume their quiet conversations in German, French. A student, lost in a thick textbook, wakes up, runs a yellow marker across several lines of *Vertebrate Zoology*.

Columbus Day in San Francisco, girls in sleeveless dresses, giggling. In a novel one of them is reading right now, someone's kissing someone someplace else than here, and in other latitudes, early frost, the sweetness of steam rising from baked apples set out on a counter to cool. Cinnamon. Chestnuts in their spiny pods ready for harvest.

The gross babble of the sweaty man, the stink, accelerate the tension of the speeding train. The passengers are nervous but deny the offense to their senses by pretending to ignore. Speaking to him might grant the man more humanity than they want, might reveal their disgust, their fear, their helplessness.

How did he get on the train?

Where is he going?

The other passengers, the clean-shaven men and fragrant young women always have someplace to go. They would never use public transportation unless they had a destination. No matter the stench, their mingled perfumes whisper, *We are leaving soon, we are leaving no matter what.*

The man steps up his offensive, stands by the doors, appearing to wait for the next stop, though his duffel bag still rests on a seat. His face smiles involuntarily, contorts, grimaces in rapid succession. His thin frame jerks and rigidifies and suddenly he turns to swat an imaginary assailant.

We feel there's hope, he might exit and leave us to our thoughts, he has so dragged us into his presence, we want his absence, he is not us, but there is something terribly familiar about him.

Like an old-fashioned train conductor, the driver announces in an eloquent, enunciated voice: "LADIES AND GENTLEMEN, THIS IS THE LAST TRANSFER POINT FOR THE FREMONT TRAIN. THE LAST TRANSFER POINT BEFORE SAN FRANCISCO."

The doors of the train car swoosh open, the man grabs his duffel bag, runs out the doors, skips back in again before the train pulls out of the station.

Again the passengers are trapped and surrounded by him, his smell occupies more space than the car. He coughs, tuberculins real and unreal spray in all directions.

A woman rushes into the car with a child in pigtails, big blue eyes, a chubby Alice in Wonderland. Tiny patent leather party shoes, flouncy white dress. The man immediately scrutinizes the child.

"Do you take good care of that baby?" he screams.

No answer.

"Bitch, bitch, the baby, I said!"

The mother hears but obeys the unspoken rule of silence established by the other passengers. Click. A psycho.

"Sit close to me, honey," she whispers, crushing the child's dress as she presses into her seat.

She would get up, child in hand, guide her daughter toward another car, but a quick survey down the aisle through the glassed door reveals no empty seats in the next car either. Cannot stand all the way into the city. "It won't be long, honey," she whispers again, clutching her purse.

Are we there yet?

"You Mexicans, you niggers, you shit!" he exhorts, pointing to three teenagers of undetermined ethnic origin applying lipstick to their soft lips. It's a school holiday and they aren't going to any parade. The girls stare at the man, then look away from him, for they too know that meeting his gaze triggers his speech.

"You you you!" he points at a large woman in a flowered dress who occupies most of a nearby double seat. "You blob, where's your ticket, where's your food stamp, hah hah hah! Go home and eat!"

The large woman gazes out into the blackness of the tunnel, her face reflecting back to her in the train car window.

Last station before San Francisco. More passengers get on. New prey. New voice over the loudspeaker garbles and swallows the announcement.

"What did he say?" German tourists say to each other in German.

"Ach, please, sir. . . ?" one musters up her guidebook English to ask the student next to her, but he couldn't make out what the driver just said, either.

The car is packed now though it's only mid-afternoon. Public holiday, sales at Macy's. Eager shoppers, confident of safety. During the big earthquake of '89, commuters felt the train jerk as if it ran over something, assumed at worst a car down the line had slipped off the track. Perhaps someone had leapt in front of the train. Tragic, awful, not personal to them.

The moment before the tumult, if anyone had looked out the window, they'd have seen it, the birds flying backward.

Today in San Francisco, there's a big Indigenous People's Parade to counter the Columbus Day event in North Beach. Several Native Americans get on the train, among them a man and a woman with a tiny baby in a carrier. They shuffle through the car looking for a spot to sit, accompanied by a large man with long black braids and one feather earring, dark Ray-Bans with mirror lenses. The car is crammed full, many passengers clutching the overhead bars. People weave in and out, separate to find any seats they can, the way they might in a crowded movie theater.

Silent for a few minutes, the man spots the Indian couple. The infant sleeps, heavily swaddled.

"What about that baby? Shut up Shut up Shut up!" he shrieks.

The baby's father glances at the man. Other passengers survey the family, confident the couple will not betray the complicity of silence. Again, the car settles down to reading, stares, whispers.

Someone can't help themselves and laughs, someone else joins in.

"Pee-pee, fuck! Shut up, I said! You're not supposed to talk." The man snickers like a naughty schoolboy, glaring at the large Indian in sunglasses whose broad, muscular shoulders give him the air of a wrestler or a nightclub bouncer.

The man stares at the bouncer's shoulders. He shakes his head, looks around.

"Hey, teepee, hey, pock face, you got tomahawks under your jacket?"

The bouncer rises.

Without excusing himself, he pushes through clumps of passengers to get to the man. "Who you talkin' to, huh?" he hovers over him. The bouncer looks down at the man's skull. The man turns his face away petulantly.

"Don't talk to me like that," the bouncer orders. "*You* shut up!" he commands and smacks the man in the face with the back of his hand.

The slap on flesh, bone echos.

With perfect choreography, neighboring passengers too close for comfort get up and float down the aisle and magically find new seats. Someone shouts out from the anonymous chorus, "Hey man, hey, leave him alone, can't you see he's a little bit . . . crazy?"

All eyes on the two men. The bouncer returns to his seat, sits up tall, invisible eyes behind the Ray-Bans. Jaws set in an expressionless face.

Anything could happen now. No BART police in sight, just fear, breathless fear. The lid is on tight. Anybody could do anything if fear had its way.

The man scowls, sinks into himself, muttering, holding his slapped cheek. Shaking, peeing. His features distorted with the humiliation of the blow, even his very stench seems to disappear.

He stands up. His urine stains a perfect circle on the carpeted floor of the train car.

The Social Contract

LATE SPRING. ANOTHER arctic week in Northern California, and humans probably caused it. Finish watching a documentary about a great opera singer of the late nineteenth century whose voice fails so he turns to silent movies. But he can't act, he fails the screen test. Boss calls with cheery news: salary just cut by twenty percent. Miserable forecast. Thankful for professional excuse to go elsewhere. I make arrangements to have a rogue shuttle service pick me up next week and take me to the airport.

I vaguely remembered the voice of the libertarian oddball owner/driver who once rattled on for the forty-five-minute drive to SFO about government and why we should get rid of it.

"I've been to junior college, you know," he said. "I'm not an uneducated person, but all these immigrants, all these people expecting the government to take care of them. It's what's bringing us down. There's got to be a stop to it."

"Oh, uh-huh," I replied, tightening my seat belt as he sped along 280 South, roadside foliage blurring in the fog.

"You're in America, hello, I mean, learn English and learn it fast. Enough bilingual education, enough coddling. I learned Vietnamese fast, I mean fast, because it was a matter of life and death, and I tell you, when you're in a foreign country, you should treat it like a matter of life and death. Did the U.S. government pay me to learn Vietnamese? No, it did not. I learned it to survive."

Uh-huh is a very useful reply in certain circumstances. Nothing but uh-huh if you can repress what might follow.

He braked hard, the sort of driver who drives right up to the car in front and if you look out the windshield, you freeze up and wish you had rosary beads. On these occasions, it's best to open a large, engaging novel and read your way to the terminal.

Except he talked, and talked, unsolicited.

"So, Berkeley, so boy, have they got opinions there. You can't get two people to agree on anything in Berkeley."

"No, I guess you can't."

"I won't put it on now, but I listen to talk radio shows day and night, that's where the real knowledge is to be had, that's where the temperature of this country is to be taken."

The day before I took off, I was anxious. I was anxious with an anxiety they used to call free floating, unattached to object, though it could have been the vague memory of the guy who was supposed to pick me up at 8 a.m. and didn't call like he said he would to confirm. I woke early and phoned the rogue service. There was a machine and the message said: "If you can't get us, call our other driver at 788-5441. His name is Mohammed."

I called Mohammed. After fifteen rings, there was no answer. I called the original number, reached the machine again, and left a message as follows:

"Hi, this is Nancy Drew. I'm calling to confirm you'll be picking me up tomorrow at 7:00 a.m. Please call me by 8:30 a.m. this morning, or I'll make other arrangements."

No one called, so around noon, I made other arrangements, this time with a straight, more expensive shuttle service. A taxi was tempting but no. The last time I called a cab in Berkeley it didn't arrive. Someone had given me last-minute tickets to the Dalai Lama at the Greek Theater. There'd be no parking with those crowds. An hour later, a man with a turban sat on the horn as I leapt down the stairs.

"I'll be late. What took you so long? It's two o'clock on Tuesday. You can't have been that busy."

"Oh," he nodded his head from side to side. "Oh lots of traffic in Berkeley. Must be a football game."

In the evening, rather late in the evening, just before I was ready to retire, the man from the rogue service phoned.

"But I'm sorry, you didn't call, thank you, I won't be needing you," I told him.

"Is that right, MA'AM!" he screamed.

"Yes it is," I said.

"Well," he exploded, "we're not open twenty-four hours a day, MA'AM," and his "ma'am" was so inflected that it sounded like it was going to blast the earpiece into the mouthpiece. It was like John Belushi but worse. This voice wasn't acting.

"Well, I'm sorry."

"Why did you make RESERVATIONS in the first place, MA'AM?" he screamed louder. "Just to cancel?"

"Listen," I said. "I need another kind of service. . . ."

"GOODbye," he slammed the receiver down.

For a while I shook at the thought of this guy coming to gun me and my kid down, rob my house while I was away, etc. Clearly a deranged vet, someone who the government should have taken care of properly, someone who got made sociopathic by the government twenty-five years ago and hasn't recovered and will never recover and will go postal very soon. Is postal already. Should be on meds. Is on too many meds. Is paranoid schizophrenic. Someone once told me, why waste time trying to psyche out lunatics. They work at it twenty-four hours a day.

Later that night, perhaps early that morning, when I had drifted off into dreamland, Ed Bradley from "60 Minutes" dropped in, popping his head into the dream as if through a door, with an earnest concerned expression. "We called the offices of blah-blah, but they would not respond to us," he announced, to me and me alone.

Then the phone rang.

"Hello," a voice said. "Are you the person who needed a ride to the airport?"

"Yes, yes," I resumed shuddering, half awake. "Why are you calling? What do you want?"

"I'm calling," the voice said, "to apologize. I'm sorry."

"Well," I said, "I'm glad you did, are, I mean, it's not very good for business, is it, to blow up at customers, I'd never recommend you now, would I? I've used your service before and been [*gulp*] satisfied, but I got anxious, I'm a very anxious person."

"Well, I'm sorry."

"Thank you for calling."

I hung up with a number of thoughts. What if everyone who'd ever wronged anyone else, anyone who'd yelled at anyone else unjustly, robbed them, hurt them—parents with children, strangers with strangers, masters with slaves, real estate developers, rich people, people who stole land from other people, etc., what if everyone who ever injured anyone else just picked up the phone and apologized?

It wouldn't help much.

Distance No Object

IN THE LARGE peach-colored room of the recently remodeled employment office, beneath a framed print of a Monet water lily, Lopo Ramírez answered every question put to him by a tired clerk who that day had already interviewed several fishmongers. The Natural Fish over in Berkeley needed a new man and they didn't want union. The clerk leaned across his glass-topped desk to hand Lopo Ramírez a blank application.

"Whatever I've done for a living," Lopo Ramírez said as he reached for the form, "after a while, I find myself having to do something else."

During the last several years, job transiency had become a commonplace pattern in anyone's career.

"We see many clients with similar job histories, Mr. Ramírez," the clerk commented disinterestedly.

Lopo Ramírez smiled, his dark milky eyes seeking a focus. It had been established in the early moments of the interview that Ramírez and the clerk shared common origins. The clerk was fluent in Ramírez's native language. But then he demurred, switching back to English with a slight defensiveness, suddenly remembering instructions from a training program he'd attended: *Keep applicant at a polite distance.* Using English, he made clear in a tone that reinforced his remove that it was his parents who came from the same country as Lopo Ramírez. But Lopo Ramírez spoke plaintively with his eyes, enormous soft pools that begged for an advocate. *Let me tell you my story*, they said, *just give me your permission, not even your enthusiasm.*

The day was waning. The amber light of late autumn seeped into the room through the half-turned blinds, casting shadows on the leaves of a large tropical plant next to the men. There were no other interviews scheduled. As Lopo Ramírez bowed his head slightly, the clerk fingered a pen and suppressed a yawn, which made the veins in his otherwise unlined forehead protrude.

"Back home, I used to fish, sir. I used to fish professionally, you know, and I stank. Forgive my frankness, sir. Every day I came home stinking, bits of fish scales stuck to my pants, threads of seaweed wrapped around my ankles. But I was young, my life was my own, and the bay was mine and the waters were warm. And I hadn't the usual impatience of youth, I was good with the nets, good with the flounder. But I stank. The smell of fish stained my fingers, it settled beneath my skin and I couldn't get rid of it. I wished I didn't stink. Believe me, I wished I could fish and not stink.

"Rosalora said she'd marry me if I quit. I quit. Then we moved to America.

"One thing led to another, as it always does.

"Now, sir, my shirt has been starched for years, my aftershave is still strong after a long day, Rosalora doesn't complain. And after all that's happened, what do I know best but fish? Granted, selling fish is different than catching fish, but I'm worthy, sir, I know the parts of a fish better than the parts of speech. And I'm experienced at standing."

How quaintly Ramírez phrased his appeal, the clerk mused. Twenty years ago this guy stuck a fishing pole out of a rowboat and now he thinks he can compete with kids half his age? Oh but these peasants are so naive when they try to sell themselves.

"Make sure you note your previous experience on the application, all right?" The clerk's smile froze as he pointed to the appropriate blanks.

"Let me tell you, sir," Lopo Ramírez insisted, "how I've incorporated my knowledge of fish with my great skill in standing. And how the two should qualify me for the very job you offer. With all. . . ."

"But I don't have the job. I mean. . . ." interjected the clerk, now irritated. He leaned across the desk, pointing again to the application. As the pitch of his voice rose, his hand shook slightly. Frustrated, then composing himself, he switched to Ramírez's native language.

"*Señor Ramírez. ¿No comprende usted?* I screen applicants for companies, I don't own the fish market. *Yo no soy el patrón.*"

"*Señor, le comprendo a usted completamente,*" Mr. Ramírez replied confidently.

The clerk sat back up straight in his chair, adjusting his glasses.

"With all due respect, sir, I'm not ignorant. I've been to night school. I try to read. And I am a patient man. I am a man who is skilled at waiting and watching. In my last job, I used to stand along the walls of a giant atrium in the middle of a museum and watch a twelve-foot circle of white rocks. Would you like to know about the Chalk Circle?"

Now the clerk sighed noticeably, no longer suppressing his fatigue. He sank into his seat, listlessly. He glanced at the hands of the pale aqua clock next to the water-lily print and decided to allow the rhythm of Ramírez's story lull him until it was time to go home.

•

White walls, grey trim, pale grey marble floors. Footsteps, brief whispers at the threshold. Clicking of the claws of black-birds, pigeons landing on the skylight—these were part of the installation I was hired to watch. And part of my days, which were installations in time. I watched them, as I once watched the sea.

Visitors often saw me as part of the installation. Imagine! A young woman dressed in black leather is leaning against the wall opposite me, close to the Chalk Circle, taking notes. Her face is fair, her lips red and shiny like varnish. She stares at me across the giant room, pretending to observe the installation, then she scribbles, her hair falls in front of her eyes, she sweeps it back, looks up at me again, returns to her notebook. She's noticed how small I am, how grey my hair has become, how dark my skin is, how I look like a hundred other men working in similar jobs.

She knows nothing about me yet she pities me. She thinks, how boring to have to stand there all day wearing a green suit and a badge! To her I am a dead end. She walks on to the colorful abstractions in the next gallery.

The rocks of the Chalk Circle were one layer deep, piled about eight inches high, all relatively uniform chunks, each per-haps six inches in diameter.

I felt I knew every rock or I didn't know any at all.

It was the light that descended from the glass panels of the atrium that gave me confidence or not. With the fish, it was the same, the light from the heavens on the waters, making them opaque or transparent.

I wasn't permitted to read while on duty, I could only walk around the room, straighten my tie, feel my wallet in my pocket, stand against a wall, bend my legs, gaze into the vents along the opposite wall, watch the hands of my watch, watch the Chalk Circle, and the visitors. My days were full and I hardly noticed them passing.

For ten minutes every couple of hours, I was relieved by another guard.

Because my English was poor, I appeared shy and ignorant, I was hired to do nothing all day but pay attention, and that served my employers who secretly believed I came from a stupid country. But really, I didn't mind what they thought, for they didn't treat me according to their thoughts.

Every night after the museum closed, the dust from the chalk had to be swept back into the circle. This was my favorite part of the job.

Once I told my supervisor that sweeping the dust into a black dustpan and carefully sprinkling it among the rocks was the moment I looked forward to every day.

My supervisor said he had to laugh. "You're a nut, Ramírez. How can you stand this job? You wetbacks have the simplest minds on earth. You just know you're almost out the door when you clean up. Listen, Ramírez, you don't have to brownnose me. Get it? Ha-ha!"

But my supervisor misunderstood the pleasure of my work, and though he was fair to me, we weren't friends on the outside because he belittled the work we did and mocked the visitors. When he spoke, I felt his gloom surround me like a fog and chill. Rosa told me, *When that happens, Lopo, put your right hand over your stomach, over your belly button, Lopo, so his bad feelings can't enter you.* Sometimes I did this if I joined him for a beer at night, but drink only increased his resentment.

He would make obscene jokes about the Chalk Circle, about the wall sculpture I usually stood next to, about another piece across the room, a large steel tube called Distance No Object. No matter how close you got to this tube, it looked far away. I had a certain fondness for it, though really, it was a predictable trick next to my Chalk Circle.

My supervisor said people were kidding themselves. He said art's not what it used to be. He said he'd worked at the museum ten years, so he supposed he knew something.

I knew nothing about art, only about the Chalk Circle.

What did art used to be? I don't think I could've guarded the Mona Lisa all day, I really don't. Could you? I think her smile would sour after a while. I think I understand why kids draw those mustaches on cheap reproductions of her, to perk her up.

The chalk rocks were so very white. Some people thought they were cold. But to me, cold is San Francisco, where the sail-boats float on a bay you can't swim in, where you go to an ocean you can only look at. It's so cold in the summer that one year I wore a turtleneck to work for a month! Sometimes if it's damp and windy, I don't even feel like looking out of the corner of my eye. If it was cold like that, I would stand where I could watch the rocks straight on. They gave off heat sometimes, like armies. Or they appeared melancholy. Some days they even looked like tall, elegant women dressed in black.

They depended on light. In the right light, white can look black, you know.

One day the artist of the Chalk Circle appeared in the atrium, standing away from it with two curators. Then the artist decided to donate the Chalk Circle to the museum. This made the cura-tors very happy, now they wouldn't have to convince the director to buy it. I was overjoyed at the news! When the exhibition was over, the museum would have to store the Chalk Circle. They would have to put the pieces into cardboard boxes with exact instructions to set them up again. I, Lopo Ramírez, wanted to stand watch over the boxes. After all, I knew those rocks better than anyone. I knew their moods and they knew mine. I could even read a book while I was guarding the rocks, because few people besides museum personnel use the archives.

Oh, I thought, then I could have a long beach of time before me every day.

But another guard, Pérez, already had the job of watching the archives. He said it was lonely work, a long shift and hardly anyone to talk to or look at. As for me, I had seen enough people, the startled expressions on their faces as they entered the atrium.

Most were too reserved to laugh, but you can tell when a person wants to and doesn't.

They didn't think my Chalk Circle was anything, some of them.

Some didn't question what it was, since it was there.

Most just walked through, never thought about it again.

But I had to live with the Chalk Circle, I had to look at it, and I tell you, it was holy.

I stared at that circle of rocks for months and I should also tell you, I was never a believer before it arrived.

One night I dreamt I had fallen asleep standing. I went to work the next morning and I actually fell asleep standing. Not from boredom, from fatigue. From practicing English verbs over and over, silently to myself, leaning against the wall in front of the Chalk Circle. In the dream, words floated by on index cards, parts of words, speaking in their own voices, fluttering away before I could pronounce them. *Repeat after me!* a word shouted. *Repeat after us!* they cried as they disappeared. . . .

How upset I was all day, not because of what happened later, but because my dream didn't come to my rescue! Dreams have been that for me often, warnings that I don't pay attention to until it's too late.

"Ramírez!" somebody was shaking me. Through the triangle of a woman's bare legs I could see my Chalk Circle way across the room. A fuzzy view of it, smaller, more horizontal.

"Ramírez, you must have passed out."

Aldo, my relief man, stood by me so close I could count his mustache hairs.

"Ramírez, get up, what's with you? Sick?"

"No, I must have dropped off and slid down."

"You hurt anything?"

"Don't think so."

"Well, amigo, you been to your locker yet?"

For a moment I couldn't connect my dream and my falling asleep on the job with something he called "locker." Sometimes the meaning of English words is delayed for me, as though several people were talking over an echo-ey loudspeaker, the sounds take time to reach me.

"Your locker, man. Check it out. You've got a nice present wrapped up in little yellow envelope, just like the rest of us."

The layoff notice did not faze me for several days. I tucked it into my shirt pocket, straightened my tie, and went back to my post. Later, when I put it on the kitchen table, Rosa glanced at it and left it under the salt shaker. It wasn't news. We all anticipated losing our jobs. A few weeks earlier, the museum had decided to contract out with a private security guard company, for a dollar an hour less. The choice was, accept less, no protection, no grievance, no benefits. Or accept nothing. Two guards quit the union then, but even my supervisor knew there was no choice for us.

Who would take our jobs? People newly arrived from my country, I guess, people who traveled a long way to find a piece of future. All they wanted was to leave their misery behind. Distance was no object to them. People with fireworks in their heads, big ideas, young dreams. But no one who would appreciate the Chalk Circle like I did.

The union settled on a little severance pay, and the last week on the job, I helped the curators disassemble the Chalk Circle. I wrapped tissue paper around each rock, placed the pieces into file boxes, labeled each box. The curators were friendly, in their way, sorry I wouldn't be staying on, but didn't know how to get personal or didn't want to. They never asked anything about me, where I came from, what I did back home. Did they assume the least of me? I never volunteered anything. They understood I knew the rocks well. And of course, as I picked each one up, held it, turned it around, why, I discovered for the first time that each piece had a different side I'd never noticed before, and every rock its own patterns. "Variegated striations," one curator said.

For a few weeks, I joined the picket line outside the museum. It was a ragtag crew, four or five unemployed security guards and a few homeless men the union hired to pad the ranks, marching around in a small circle, singing sad union songs. A few photographers stopped to take pictures, and sometimes a young person would lean against a stone pillar and give us the peace sign.

"Ramírez!" one of the curators I especially liked called out the first morning. "I'm sorry. Normally I wouldn't cross a picket line, but I've got so much work, you know. . . . I've got to help hang that big Salgado show, I. . . ."

"It's okay, Mr. Rosen, it's okay, we're out here to stop visitors, not workers. Hey, say hello to Distance No Object for me, Mr. Rosen."

"What's that Ramírez?" Mr. Rosen shouted back, as he pulled open the heavy brass door and disappeared into the lobby.

•

The pale aqua clock on the wall of the employment office struck five, and as the clerk stood up, he closed the file in front of him and straightened his glasses with both hands. "Thank you for coming in, Mr. Ramírez. We'll be sure to call if the fish market wants an interview."

Lopo Ramírez also stood up and held out his hand to shake the clerk's. The clerk did not notice as he turned from his desk to switch off the lights.

SWAT

JULY. BRIGHT COLD 9 A.M. before the fog lifts over Berkeley. It appears to be summer only by the calendar. Could be spring in Antarctica, the woman thinks, crossing the street against the light. Her child's dirty fleece jacket is zipped to the chin. A mist encloses the city as though there were nothing outside it, no horizon. The fog walls off drivers driving to work, the few people walking down University Avenue toward the Employment Development Commission.

Berkeley is a small city with no boulevards. No grand promenades, no serious pedestrian traffic. University Avenue, gateway to a world-class university, is the only true four-lane street. The school is nestled at the upper reaches of the avenue at the base of the hills behind lush landscape. No sign announces the campus to the visitor. At the westerly reaches of the town, just east of I-80, under the overpass where there are no trees, homeless and taggers mark their turf. In the moonlight, shopping carts rest near the Amtrak tracks like abandoned train cars. Above, pimps and crack heads pock the night. Between these unpaired parentheses, a mile of liquor stores with big parking lots, the Bel Air Motel, Big O Tires, auto parts, fast burgers, the Hawaiian Temple Bar. A few years ago, the Bangladeshis and the Pakistanis moved in. Now the street is thriving—the Maharani Restaurant, Bombay Bazaar, "Computer" Saris, and plenty of copy stores.

Should be renamed G. Mahatma Gandhi Way, the woman thinks, as she buttons her jacket at the collar.

There's a line of men outside the employment office meandering around a scrawny cypress, up against the red brick, sucking breakfast from containers nested in paper bags. The woman tightens her hold on her child's hand. Her eyes are averted, her peripheral vision sharp from city life. She is past the age acceptable to men, but they stare at her with bloodshot eyes anyway. Mother and daughter step around glass shards, bottle caps, candy wrappers, vials.

The child's braid bounces as she skips around the men to the door.

Inside the fluorescence of the Employment Development Commission, two children sit on folding chairs facing a long snaky line of unemployed grownups standing in front of Information.

A clerk whispers to herself as she types, *Date of birth, 2-26-67, Last name, H-a-r-r-i-s-o-n, Address, 2-6-2-5 F-i-f-t-h S-t.*

"Next!"

A tiny toddler with pom-pom pigtails, plump cheeks and thighs sits motionless. An older child is swinging his thin legs, flip-flops flopping, staring into the pale pink wall next to him, at a blue water-lily print. Someone changed the picture since he was last here, last year. A grownup presses in a secret code and a door opens. For a moment the older child leans forward to glimpse the vast interior office, a space ten times the size of the outside waiting area, filled with empty desks, computer terminals, files. Three or four silent clerks circulate in the silence. The door slams, metal echoes. The children sit unattended by an adult for a long time, leaning on each other's shoulders.

People leave the lines, sit down, a name is called, and sometimes a person mysteriously disappears into the interior room. When the older child leans forward to watch the people disappear, the younger one is thrown off balance, then his body rights itself quickly.

"Red Toyota station wagon, red Toyota station wagon," a security guard paces the length of the waiting room, warning the unemployed. "Whoever's the driver of the red Toyota station wagon, put some money in the meter, right away."

"You go sit down with those other children," the unemployed woman tells her daughter. The girl carries a big book with puppies and dogs on the cover and sits down in the row behind the other children. The mother admonishes her, tells her to sit so she can see her.
"You see those two kids?"
The daughter nods.
"You see how quiet and well-behaved they are?"
She nods again.
"Maybe they want to see your book too. Go sit next to them."

The toddler moves over and makes space for the girl. She opens her dog book, insists on turning the pages, holds on to them tightly, demands they all look at the dalmatians, her current favorite.

The daughter runs back and forth to her mother, asking questions. The other children don't move. "Why don't these puppies have any spots, Mommy? Can I have a peppermint? When will we leave? What are you doing? What does this spell—E-N-T-E-R?" Her fingers trace the letters on a sign attached by rope to poles on stands. She tries to sit down on the rope, but the poles wiggle, threatening to topple.

The daughter tugs at her mother's purse, and her mother tells her to stop because she has to write and what happens when you stand too close to someone when they're writing? The little girl crawls under the counter and opens her book. The mother asks her to sit back down next to the well-behaved children.

At last, the mother is at the head of the Information line, states her business, is given more papers. She leans in to fill them out at the counter, is assigned a number and told to go sit down again and wait until called. She sits down for another wait. The daughter is restless, wants a drink of water, wants to go potty.

To go potty means what if they call her number while.

They go potty.

Mother and daughter sit down again in the row behind the well-behaved children.

A man sits down at the end of the row, leaving several seats between himself and the toddler. Bloodshot eyes. The children turn to him but don't speak.

The unemployed woman offers the children peppermints, how old are you, how old is she.

"He's a boy," the father says.

"Oh I'm sorry," the woman says.

"They're so well behaved," she says.

The father doesn't answer. Stares straight ahead.

"Yes," a lady in a crocheted hat nods. "That's the way we like them."

The lady's number is called. She rises and the contents of her purse spill out onto the linoleum floor. "I'm twenty-seven!" she yells. "That's me, I'm twenty-seven, and I'm coming as fast as I can!"

She bends to scoop up her things and her glasses fall off her head but at last she hurries to the counter. In a moment, she returns, sits down again, and rummages in her purse for a pen.

"Green Oldsmobile with tinted windows, green Olds with tinted windows. The meter maid is up the street," the security guard calls out again.

"Do you go to kindergarten?" the unemployed mother asks the oldest well-behaved child.

"Yes, and I'm going to college. I'm going to be a policeman. I'm going to be a SWAT man."

"Well," says the little girl, "I'm going to be a meter maid. Not! We hate meter maids, we hate them!"

The lady in the crocheted hat turns around. "Well, I was a meter maid," she snarls, her glasses low on her nose.

"You seem like a perfectly nice woman," says the unemployed mother.

"It's not me, it's the city, the city, do you hear?" says the lady in the crocheted hat. "They're the mean ones!"

"Why have they gotten so mean?" the unemployed mother asks.

"I don't know," she says. "Anyway, I just did it on call, part time, you know. When they called me," she says to the little girl who hates meter maids.

11 a.m. The summer sun burns through the fog and heats up the room. The unemployed mother plays a belly-button game with the children. They're sweaty, their legs stick to the metal seats. The room is filled now, airless from anticipation, boredom.

As soon as the unemployed mother offers the children a peppermint, each of them clamors for another.

One child tickles the other, giggles, the other tickles the other, and the littlest tickles the unemployed mother.

"You three are puppies," she laughs.

"We're not puppies!" they protest. "We're kids."

"We come a long way here," the oldest boy volunteers.

"Did you come on a freeway?"

"Dunno."

"Did you drive?"

"Yes."

"What's the name of your school?"

"Kindergarten."

"Yeah, he's going into first grade," the father says, his eyes on the toddler. "*This one* don't talk, he won't talk till his birthday. He's twenty-two months."

"This is fun," the older one says. "Can I have my birthday here?" he asks the unemployed mother.

"Well," she says, "this is no place for a birthday."

"But there's candy," he says, "you've got candy."

He gives a huge smile, points at new people coming and going, their children taking phone books off the shelves, knocking over chairs.

The unemployed mother pretends to poke her pen in each child's navel.

"You have one, and you have one, and you have one."

"Do it again!" they giggle.

Their giggles accelerate, the toddler gets off his chair and snuggles against the woman. "You have one," she says softly. He lifts his shirt and giggles.

"You have one too." The older child giggles.

The father suddenly gets up and walks over to the toddler, jerks his fat arm and smacks him on the bottom.

Smack! against the paper diaper makes a popping sound.

"You behave, you sit down, do you hear?" the father mutters. "I'm talking to YOU!"

The little child waddles over to an empty row of folding chairs, climbs onto one, and sits. The metal vibrates and echoes slightly down the row. The child's face contorts, his chest heaves. There are no tears. He is silent.

The father sits down and stares at the counter. The lady in the crocheted hat turns around and nods in approval.

Giggles die back.

Crime and Punishment

I WAS CRUISING HOME after a late movie and a glass of wine with an old friend. I was in no particular hurry, just carried along by the beat of Paul Simon's "Graceland," window rolled down, and the night breeze fluffing my hair. In the film, which was very French and cool, the women were bored, even capricious with the emotions of the men, playing with them just to pass the time until something better came along. The men tried earnestly to woo the women, first with surprises, then with logic, but the French women beat them at their own game.

It was close to midnight. The streets of Berkeley were empty. Paul Simon was singing that *"losing love was like a window in your heart, everybody knows you're blown apart, everybody sees the wind blow. . . ."*

I was thinking that I wasn't so sure about that, though it sounded poetic. I've noticed that people tend to take you for what you say about yourself, and more and more they're less interested in how you feel or what's happened to you.

It was getting chilly so I rolled up the window and cranked up the sound.

Suddenly, red lights flashed in my rearview mirror like a hundred Christmas trees.

Groaning, I pulled over and rolled down my window before the officer got out of his car. He was slow about it, pretty short for a cop, thin, pale-faced, with a few pimples and a lot younger than me.

"Know why I stopped you, ma'am?" he said in a flat *Dragnet* tone. He didn't look at me directly but with one of those gazes that if you followed it, you would feel you were sitting about a foot to the side of yourself. I think people used to call it "wall-eyed."

"You were doing thirty-nine in a twenty-five-mile residential zone."

Crime of crimes, I thought. Where were you last month when that uninsured motorist smashed into me? Why aren't you out looking for muggers? But a wave of contrition overtook me about not actually knowing how fast I was going. I like to be conscious of my transgressions.

"I'm sorry," I said softly, not wanting to open my mouth too wide because he might smell the wine on my breath.

I handed over my license before he asked for it.

"You ever been cited before for speeding?"

"Never," I said. Never in California, I squirmed, hoping I was telling the truth, because it was easy enough for him to find out. By now the statute of limitations had surely run out on my teenage crimes.

"I'm sorry," I said again, trying to throw my voice like a ventriloquist while keeping my lips together but not too together.

He shined his flashlight on my license and peeked inside my car.

"Alone? It's pretty late."

"I'm too old for curfew," I smiled.

"Well, you seem like a good person," he said.

My smile was beginning to irritate me like a stiff collar. How could he come to such an assessment from such a brief encounter? Of course, Berkeley cops are famous for their mustaches, longish hair, and sensitivity training. "We have to be alert to cultural differences," an officer once comforted us when the neighborhood complained about the unreported robberies at the liquor store across the street, the crack addicts with their Uzis, and the owners with their .45's not too hidden behind the counter.

I am a good person, I thought, and while I have broken the law, I have not broken it very much.

"You're from Berkeley, huh? You're probably well educated. You're probably sophisticated. Are you sophisticated?"

"Well, I suppose you could say that, but it's usually a word you don't use on yourself."

"Oh is that right?" he said. "I didn't know that." There was genuine curiosity in the tone of his voice, no sarcasm.

"So how do you use it?"

"Well, you might call someone else sophisticated, like you called me, I mean, you used it right. . . ."

"So, you seem sophisticated, or maybe you just don't like to toot your own horn. That's good," he said. "Modesty is a virtue, you know. Should I give you a ticket?" he asked. "What would you do if you were me?"

I did not know why I seemed sophisticated to him. I was wearing blue jeans and a T-shirt and driving an old Datsun. I certainly knew I did not want eight hours of sick yuk-yuks in comedy traffic school, steeper insurance premiums, etc. Of course, I didn't think all of this in so many words, I just thought No Ticket. Not Want Ticket.

"Well, I, ah. . . ."

"Think of it this way," he said. "Do you deserve a ticket?"

My smile blew out like a lightbulb. This was a moral inquiry. Was I guilty enough to deserve punishment? Now he was asking me an ethical question, perhaps with metaphysical consequences.

I'll admit, being a little drunk and not wanting to show it

forces you to focus a little too hard on the immediate. I wondered if he could tell, if he was just playing with me. I pondered the word "deserve."

"What do you think? You've been loose with the pedal foot, you've been tooling along—and by the way, your stereo was way too loud—and not paying any regard for the fact that people live on this street."

He slapped the roof of my car. "People live here," he insisted, "so they could be coming home and parking and crossing the street. And you could be failing to see them. You have, in effect, robbed these residents of their right to safety. I'll bet most speeders don't think of themselves as thieves, do they?"

"No, that's the first I've heard of it, officer. You've created the perfect metaphor."

"Metaphor, that's right. Like *Time Bandits*, huh? Of course it's late and your subconscious probably thought, 'Hey, I can just drive like I want 'cause there's no one around. I can just do what I like, I own the road.' But now that I've stopped you, you'll drive along this street and soon you'll come to a commercial zone, and you'll have to slow down, there'll be a light. . . ."

"Well," I said, trying to be fair, "you could give me a warning citation."

"Let me put it this way," he ignored my offer and cleared his throat. "Should I ticket you? Objectively speaking, should I ticket you? What would you do if you were me?"

"I don't know," I said. "If I were you . . . I'm a college professor."

"Well," he jumped in immediately, "what if one of your students cheated on a test?"

"I don't know, I don't know," I said, stuttering, not sounding like a college professor at all. "I don't know what you should do. I don't give tests. I teach poetry."

"Oh," he said, "poetry. Well, what if one of your students turned in some writing and you knew it wasn't theirs, say it was by Hemingway, you knew the passage. . . ."

Hemingway, I thought, hardly wrote poetry, but I wasn't in a position to defend genre just now.

"Well," I said, "once I taught in a jail and an inmate used a piece of a poem by Walt Whitman. I was so astounded that I didn't even call him on it. I mean, he had memorized Whitman!"

"Is that so?" the policeman said, rubbing his eye underneath his glasses. "Those cons, they'll take anything. But about you? Have you decided? About the ticket?"

I was growing impatient, even irritable, and exceedingly sober. I was made to understand that I would be responsible for my own ticket. I did not want to be responsible. It was enough work to have to pump one's gas, bus one's dishes, unload one's groceries onto the conveyer belt at the grocery store, etc. I envisioned a world where criminals, real criminals, went before judges who would impose the extra burden of making them sentence themselves—given the options, so to speak—will that be five years at hard labor or leg irons and solitary? I did not like such options, I did not like having to choose . . . I wanted someone else who had some authority in his field—the field of moving violations—to actually make a judgment so at least I could protest it if I wanted or accept it. I grew up in a world of protest—where did that go? Where was the hard edge of pompous authority to butt up against? I wondered if this cop was lazy, just part of a growing generation of lazy people who did not want to make decisions or exert authority because they were afraid you might not like them. The anxiety of making the wrong choice overtook me. I recalled images of people saying the wrong thing and then having to dig their own graves. Only, I had the chance to say I didn't want to. *Just give me the fucking ticket*, I thought, *just ticket me.*

"Well, I tell you what," he smiled. "I tell you what, you were polite, you were honest, you didn't give me a hard time."

"Oh," I said, "people give you a hard time?"

"Oh yeah," he said. "Oh yeah. You bet they give me a hard time. I stop 'em, they bad-mouth me, some of these kids. They talk like devils, some of these kids, you know, from Oakland. . . ."

"Oh," I said, "that's absurd."

"Absurd, yeah, now that's a word. Is that a word Hemingway would use?"

"I don't know."

"Well, you're the professor. Is that a Hemingway word?"

"It could be. It very well could be."

Sleepy

after Chekhov

LATE AFTERNOON. WINTER sun muted by fog. Three older women at a metal table in the ice cream shop, their hands cupped around steaming cups. Marissa, the clerk, a woman of twenty, is rocking a stroller in which her baby is curled, asking a little girl at the counter what she'll have.

The shop is brightly lit. On a shelf behind the counter, a row of Italian soda syrups, two baby bottles, a pink pacifier reflected in the plate mirror. The phone is ringing. The baby is crying, a low consistent cry. A few more customers enter and the bells on the door handle jingle. It is very warm. There is a smell of dried milk and perfume in the air.

The baby continues to cry, not a cry of alarm, not hunger. The baby cries a cry of sleepiness. And Marissa is tired. Her eyes are burning, her head droops, her neck aches. She feels as though her face is glued to her bones.

The little girl at the counter asks for a dish of mango and lemon sorbet. Marissa pushes the stroller back and forth with her foot while scooping out the ice cream. When she puts the cup on the counter, the girl's fair face turns red.

"No," the girl says to her mother. "I didn't want mango ice cream, I wanted mango sherbet."

"Tell her," the mother whispers. "Tell her what you want."

Marissa repeats what the child orders. The dull look on her face contrasts with the sweetened tone of her voice. "You want mango sorbet, is that it, honey?"

She reaches for another cup. The baby cries louder as Marissa moves down the row of ice cream canisters, bending into them, scooping out the sorbet.

The three women at the table stare and whisper to themselves.

When the mother pays for the sorbet, Marissa offers her the rejected cup.

"Do you eat ice cream? I won't charge you for it, I'll just have to throw it away."

The mother reluctantly takes the ice cream.

Marissa is the only clerk in the shop during her shift. The store is a part of a small national chain that wasn't doing very well until the regional director added an espresso machine and pastries. After the baby came, Marissa was strolling by and saw a Help Wanted sign in the window. She had stayed home with her older child, then the county cut her off. Not many people want ice cream in the winter, she reasoned to herself when she applied for the job. It'll be easy. Today she had to bring the baby to work because her neighbor couldn't look after her.

The mother and the little girl sit down across from the clerk and her baby and start to giggle.

"And when I came home, guess what I saw?"

"I can't guess," says the little girl, swirling the two sorbets together with a tiny plastic spoon.

"I looked out the window and there were two Anna's hummingbirds at the feeder. Two! And a big blackbird perched on your swing!"

"Four and twenty blackbirds. . . ."

"Did you know that the tiniest hummingbird in the world is this big?" the mother says, holding her forefinger and thumb parallel. "And its wings beat so fast that you can't even seem them?"

"If you can't see them, how do you know they're there, Mommy?"

Someone pushes the door open and suddenly the shop is filled with smell. Marissa cannot see the white floor tiles tracked with mud and cat shit. She can only see a large woman with red sores on her face, thin grey hair sticking out of a cap like pencil marks.

The sounds of the mother and child giggling and talking seem far away and make Marissa drowsy. Marissa sees her father scraping his boots, her mother shaking a rag at him.

"Why don't you wipe your damn shoes off before you come into the house? What's the matter with you?"

"I'm hungry. What you got?"

"What do you think this is, a restaurant? Where were you for dinner?"

Marissa rocks her baby, wants a cigarette, shuts her eyes. Her father is rising from his own ashes, hovering over her, smiling. Her brother has just telephoned her with the news, Daddy is dead. It looks like he's been dead for a couple of days. His face is swollen, like something burst inside. Marissa rocks the baby, remembers the telephone call stopped her heart for a second and it's never beat properly again. Even the doctor who delivered her first baby said so, said there was something irregular.

"You should be careful about getting pregnant again," he told her. "Are you sexually active? Why don't we put you on the pill?"

She sees her father in the hospital. "What a wonderful place," he tells her. "The meals are terrific, the nurses are nice to me, I watch television all day and don't have to work. It's a vacation!"

She sees her cousin Olivia shaving her legs in the sink, fresh from detox, holed up at a hotel in downtown Oakland, just after her fourth kid.

"Jail's not so bad, you know, they feed you and you don't have to pay rent and men don't hustle you, you know."

Marissa takes the bus to Chico to go to her father's funeral, but there is no funeral, just the end of a man, a police report. Cause of death: natural.

"Marissa," she hears a man yell. The manager of the ice cream shop is standing over her baby.

"What is this, Marissa? Why is this baby here? What is this mess on the floor? Get the mop, Marissa, immediately. This is a violation of health codes, you want the health department to shut us down? What are you doing? You can't bring a baby to work! You're spaced out. Don't you understand how to do your job?"

Marissa pops up, rushes to the back room to get the bucket, fills it at the spigot. The rushing water fills her ears, rushing over the mop like a waterfall. She grabs the mop. The baby is wailing, wailing. Marissa swabs down the floor. The woman who tracked in the mess is at the counter, tapping her fingernails, clearing her voice in an exaggerated *ah hem*.

Marissa sees her mother in a dirty flannel nightgown, wringing her hands. "It should have been me instead of him, the bastard," she moans.

"What about my coffee crunch fudge? I've been waiting forever. I have the money right here," the woman slaps a fat baggie of pennies on the counter.

The manager serves her.

Marissa picks up the baby and sticks a bottle of premixed formula in her mouth. The baby sucks, spits out the nipple, its tiny hands trembling.

"Are you asleep or what?" the manager yells. "The counter needs washing, the bathroom is filthy, look at this scooper—how can you let all this pile up?"

Marissa stares at the manager, rocking her baby in her arms.

"You know, I had a feeling about you when you walked in here. You're a welfare brat, you don't know shit about working. Why don't you just go home and tend to your damn babies. Tell the county you can't work, you don't know how to work."

Marissa puts the baby back into the stroller. She runs hot water and disinfectant over a large sponge and scalds her hands picking it up. She sponges down the counter and thinks how nice it would be to lay down on the sponge. And all at once, the sponge grows, swells, fills up the whole shop. She drops the sponge, shakes her head, and tries to look at things so that they don't grow big.

"Marissa, sweep the sidewalk in front. Take the bottles out back to the recycling. The entryway is disgusting, it's filled with litter, customers will think we're closed."

The baby is still crying. Marissa props open the door to sweep the sidewalk.

The manager sneers, apologizes to the customers inside about the rush of cold air.

"You are so stupid," he says to her as she returns the push broom to the back room. "You're no good for business, even in Berkeley. What are you going to do about that baby?"

"I'm sorry. It won't happen again. Please, I need this job."

"You need a job, you do it right. You're not all here, Marissa. You've already taken too much time off. I need someone reliable."

The manager puts the day's receipts into a zipper bag and rushes off to the bank. Marissa is alone again in the shop. The baby has never stopped crying. Dusk is falling, her eyes burn, she could fall asleep standing. The shop has emptied out. She lowers the blinds, rearranges the chairs at the tables. She dumps the coffee, starts a fresh pot, pulls a box of sugar packets from the shelf and refills the sugar dishes.

At dark, a few teenagers blast in. One wants a milkshake, another a sundae.

"You got toppings? Hey how come you don't got toppings? What kind of place is this?"

"Oh, what a darling baby. She yours?"

Marissa nods.

"Boy, you is a sourpuss, isn't you? Why don't you smile a little? You supposed to be makin' people happy serving ice cream."

"You got fries? I want fries. Hey, miss, I'm talkin' to you. . . ."

One of the teenagers glances around the empty shop. "Where's the bathroom?"

Marissa reaches for a wooden block with a key and nods in the direction of the restroom in back.

She is scooping out the chocolate ice cream for the double chocolate fudge sundae one of the teenagers ordered. She feels something poking her ribs.

When she looks up, there's a boy with a gun pressing into her side.

"Okay, empty the register," he says quietly.

Marissa reaches for her baby. The stroller is empty. One of the teenagers is holding the baby like a platter, cooing at her.

"Aren't you a little doll? Ooh-wee. I wish I had one like you." She swings the baby to and fro.

The baby is quiet for the first time all day. "What a sweet little thing. Now you see, all it wanted was to be held. We walked in here and Miss Sourpuss couldn't get her baby down. No wonder. This baby knows."

"Maybe we should take this baby home? Whatcha think? She

don't seem a fit mother, bringing a baby in here. Maybe we should report her to child protective services."

Marissa stands frozen, her lips pursed to scream, unable to make a sound.

"Okay okay, just hurry it up, get the cash out of that box."

"All right but there's nothing in it. The manager took the money to the bank an hour ago."

"Listen you bitch, there's gotta be something in there. What do you care? It's not your money. Open it up."

He presses the pistol harder into her side.

Marissa punches in the code for a sundae and $3.75 on the keypad and the drawer opens. A few singles, a couple of fives, change.

"Hand it over," the teenager says.

She takes the bills out of the register and shoves them at the boy.

"The change, the change too. "

As she scoops the change out of the drawer, the quarters flip onto the floor, some into a bucket of strawberry sorbet.

"You clumsy shit! Pick up that change," another teenager orders her.

Marissa stoops to the floor, and the boy with the gun stoops with her as though they were attached by the gun. The coins stick to the sticky floor.

"Come on, come on, let's get out of here."

She drops the quarters into the pocket of her apron. When she's picked up the coins, she rises and the boy with the gun rises with her.

"Okay, now take off that apron and hand it over."

Marissa slowly unties the bow and pulls the apron off, one eye on the girl holding her baby. The shop is quiet, except for the hum of the refrigerator reverberating from the back room.

"So let's see what else is under that apron," one of the boys says.

"Yeah, let's have it."

"Nah, I don't want it," another boy says. "Nasty snatch, she's pretty ugly."

"Take it off," the boy with the gun points the gun to her skirt.

Marissa stands behind the counter naked from the waist down. One of the teenagers laughs, grabs the apron from the boy with the gun and stuffs it under his leather jacket. The girl holding Marissa's sleeping baby puts her down gently on one of the tables. The boy with the gun looks at Marissa and begins firing into the ice cream, one shot at a time into every canister. When he reaches the end of the row, he turns and aims and turns away.

The bells on the door of the shop clatter and clank as he grabs for the handle.

The Stick

HOW SHE LOVED HIM, before language. Photographs reveal two infants clinging to the bars of a crib, their chubby faces hanging over the rail, their tiny bodies shoulder to shoulder. His roan brown hair to her wheat color.

He was a lanky stick of a child, legs to neck, a snake with feet. Soft, loose-limbed, quiet, polite, a grownup's dream with his may-I-be-excused at the table. He would not risk a move on the court or the slopes that he imagined might put him in jeopardy. As a toddler, he clung to his father's legs at the appearance of strangers. She flew into their arms. She was small, fierce, compact, a current ran through her, compelling action, and this physical mandate often caused her to forget social manners that she had learned at three; a careless carefree flinging of turtlenecks, socks, twisted jeans on the bedroom floor, bags of stuffed animals from a recent trip still unpacked, the limbs of teddy bears and dogs and dolls spilling off the sides of the suitcase. Wadded-up paper treasures, coins, beads under her bed. Often a knotted tangle in the back of her hair. "So what, you care too much about appearances," she told her fastidious mother. Never asked for new clothes, lived in a tiny cell of a bedroom, nest-like for a young child but crowded by girlhood, until the mother begged to move her to another.

Tiny rosettes of breast began to form on her early as though they were separate from her. When she noticed them, she rummaged through a box of hand-me-downs and pulled out the training bras. This development she treated with pragmatism, a need easy to satisfy for now, like so many of her needs.

He complained, she did not, though both suffered from allergies and the usual aches of childhood. He gave no thought to friends, always had them, across the street, at school. He was liked. Organized sports brought him into contact with other boys his age with whom he spent time on the weekends, taking for granted their friendship—a simple entitlement. She fretted, analyzed her position among her friends, craved a one-and-only best one, one to whom she could tell her secrets and be assured of secrecy. She fought for the love of certain girls, at once feeling herself on the fringe of the inside clique as well as too good for it. An elaborate social structure of inner circles and outer circles and offshoots of groups seemed in place at school—she was part of the very circle she yearned for, though she imagined herself outside it. There was a girl she thought at the center, and it was this girl's love and notice that she craved and rejected. For it meant loyalty to a dictatorial child and perhaps subservience, which her character could not guarantee.

Until recently, she puzzled over distinctions made between girls and boys. She would often play with boys, reprimanded by other girls for doing so, insisting boys would not betray her the way girls might. Or they had no capacity for the kind of harsh gossip she watched other girls engage in. There had been "couples" since the second grade, so and so are boyfriend and girlfriend, which meant that both parties announced their interest and status. Nothing more. Too-too young for dates. But with girls, if one revealed privately to another that she liked a boy, she expected the information to go no further and, of course, it did, quickly and deliriously, from the top of the schoolyard stairs, broadcast and humiliating.

He had no sense of such behavior. If it occurred around him, he was oblivious to it.

"I don't just like him," she announced. "I like-like him. You know," she smiled coyly. Sitting next to each other in the backseat of the car, they gabbed, joked, she invoked characters from the book she was reading, he offered counterparts from a recent movie, giggles arose, and they were mutual. She agreed with him, she disagreed equally, offering him a box of juice, and did he know the words to the song from *The Titanic?* If not, she would sing them. And she did. He listened; the topic changed; she decided to read him a passage from *Black Beauty*. He gazed out the car window at the moving traffic.

The pond was visible from the road to the horse ranch, and in winter migrating ducks, blue herons startled the passerby. Holsteins and Jerseys grazed the green hills that held the valley like a cupped hand. The deep croaking voices of frogs that lived in the gullies and ponds nearby filled the valley with their strange music. The children led their horses out of the stalls; three or four ranch dogs trotted alongside hoping to sneak into the arena.

Once inside the gate, fear paralyzed the boy's will. The girl rode off like a heroine, her hair flying from beneath her helmet, the sound of her laughter echoing off the mirrors of the arena.

He stood still against the rails, dazzled by her. She squeezed her horse's flanks slightly with her strong calves and whispered; the gelding took off in a perfect trot. She lifted her pelvis equally perfectly to post with his rhythms. With each lift, she thrust her chest forward slightly. When she rounded the back of the arena, she saw the boy from the distance. As always, he was not really watching her but inside himself, his eyes in her direction, gazeless.

"Aren't you going to ride with me?" she shouted.
"Nah, I'll just watch today. I don't want to ride," he feigned.
"Let's go to the pond when I'm finished, okay?" she said. She cantered off, her trainer irritated with this impetuosity.
"I didn't give you permission to canter!" the trainer yelled. "Ease into a walk, now, sitting trot first. Let's see a smooth transition."

The girl peeled her sweatshirt off to her bathing suit, told the boy to do the same, and ran toward the bank of the pond, leaving him by the weathered picnic table. He picked at the splintery wood, he looked down at the muddy grasses of the marsh. He could hear her calling him from beyond a grove of live oaks; a scrub jay screeched nearby. Cabbage whites fluttered, a giant horse fly buzzed and landed on his shoulder. He flicked it away. The last milkweed blooms of spring, protected into summer by the overhanging trees and the cool lush of the bog, blew off their stems in a sudden wind that died back as quickly as it had arisen. A creature plopped into the pond; then another; a dog followed with a deeper splash; ripples disturbed the banks.

She crouched down beside a raised mound to examine a trail of ants importing breadcrumbs into the colony. Then she leapt up and sat on a nearby rock, folding her tanned legs under her body. She felt a tiny poke, then a soft scratching between her shoulder blades, lifting the criss-cross straps of her bathing suit. She turned abruptly. He sat two or three feet behind her, holding a long forked stick. She stayed still, allowing him to move the stick across her back, down her spine, up again beneath her flaxen hair. The stick caught a few strands and he jerked it away.

"Owwwww!" she cried. "Stop it! Let go!"

He dropped the stick, leapt up, and ran off. She ran after him, angry, determined to hit him.

When she caught him, her cheeks flushed, eyes squinting, no words emerged from her mouth. They looked at one another, he was afraid she might strike him. She lifted her leg as if to begin a kung fu kick, and held it midair and let it drop to the floor of the embankment. He skirted to the side of her to retrieve the stick.

"Don't you dare!" she yelled. "I'll get you, I'll get you!" She was furious. "Payback time is near! Payback no punches!" she declared.

He grabbed the stick, threw it down on the ground in front of her.

"Here, you can have it, if you want it. It's just a stupid stick."

But she didn't pick it up. She kicked at it, she scowled, seething at the whirl of sensations inside her. The pleasure of the stick across her spine, the strange new tingle, suddenly turning to pain.

On the way home from the stables, she did not speak to him. They sat apart, on opposite sides of the car, each with an arm resting on a window, the wind scattering their hair, backpacks between them. She leaned her face out the window, and the fast highway air made her eyes tear up.

Where She Stays

AT SIXTEEN SHE HAD shown signs of unhappiness. Not the acute, ordinary kind that throws itself on the bed and sobs over a broken romance or a friend's betrayal, but a sadness she wore quietly like a simple dark shift. In the busyness of the household, it seemed her character. The other children were buoyant, student body president and lacrosse captain, A's and Ivy futures. Lila was "artistic," without much art to show for it. There had been family money once, now just the aspirations of a wide-lawned, comfortable class.

I loved Lila. I felt I'd known her before she was born. When she was small, I commissioned paintings from her, told her I was her first "dealer." I had no children of my own, and a long-dissolved marriage drew me closer to the family, and they considered me one of them. My gallery work took me East frequently and I always stayed with them.

Lila's mother Mara and I met at Berkeley. Even in college, people confided in her more than she confided in them. I felt close to her, and she was as close as a wife and mother with three children can be to an old friend. She was always warm, well adjusted, popular, yet private. She treated everyone with equanimity, kindness. Her early marriage endured, seemingly unruffled by serious dissent or ambition.

Evidence at age seventeen, from a diary left on the coffee table:

High today, no tomorrow. History less of a bloody blur, in English class, Keats so beautiful, I like him better than Shelley with all those hysterical exclamation marks. Floating through the halls, felt good, and no telltale pot breath.

A year later, Mara found a needle in Lila's purse. Nothing but the ugly squat hypodermic, a fearful interrogation, and Lila's lies. *Only sometimes, not a lot, not hooked, can take it or leave it.* Later in the year, an overdose just short of gone.

We drove, Mara and I, several hours to the country, to the halfway house where Lila stayed after detox.

The literature from the foundation offered the now standard method of rehabilitation—in order to get cured you have to be out of your element. The golden rule: Change People, Place, and Things. The pace was one day at a time; otherwise, the days would add up to the crushing thing called life, and no one there was prepared to imagine the future.

Each day was packed with group meetings, therapy, chores, structure. There were counselors on site, but the residents prepared food themselves, large quantities of it. Every day they went to the minimart in the small village up the road; they did not make lists of what they needed. They bought chips and sodas and cigarettes and shampoo and movie magazines, and were treated well by the townspeople. Everybody knew about the house, and though the women didn't stay more than a few months, with fifteen or twenty steady shoppers, the town council was happy.

The road to the halfway house was dotted with small Pennsylvania Dutch towns, meager-looking places badly in need of paint and commerce. We stopped several times because our instructions weren't clear. Mara rolled down the window at a light to ask two local women who looked related, with their tightly curled colorless hair.

"Oh dear," the driver said, "I don't know. I've lived around here all my life, but the road changes."

She became flustered, jutting her chin forward and squeezing her eyes. The woman in the passenger seat stared ahead.

"Just get on Highway 22 and you'll find it."

We pulled over at an auto parts store, signaling to a man and a son in a truck. The man rolled down his window, a huge face dotted with blistery patches, and a beard down to his stomach.

"Just get on Highway 17 and go past the interchange and stay on the road and take the Charm exit."

We took off again, but couldn't find a Charm exit, so we stopped at a convenience store. Everyone in line looked like they slept with each other and produced a directional deficiency in their offspring.

"Ever wonder why people are so unattractive in these places?" I tried to distract Mara.

She was silent, she only wanted company, not conversation. Lila's breakdown had turned her insomniac. Sleeping pills, tranquilizers suddenly in her medicine cabinet. It was the incomprehensibility of it all. The why that could not be answered by examining the consequences. An algebra with an x never solved. And the shame, not the ancient shame a child used to bring to a family, but a personal shame like a nausea. Lila had a sickness, and Mara now felt a version of it.

The plan was for her to take Lila out for a meal while I stayed at the house with a book to keep me occupied. Lila had improved, her counselor said, but she had a long way to go.

The light was grim and grey, held by a heat that formed a second skin around our bodies as we drove. Such summer heat in the

East always dissolved into rain, like a person with a taut, troubled mind might burst into tears. The highway was lined with fields of tiny cornstalks, two feet high, and after the storm passed, the corn seemed to grow right before our eyes.

We drove up to a large old farmhouse, surrounded by old maples. A few cottages in back, a single towel hanging on a long clothesline. A weathervane, still in the still heat. Lila appeared, freshly made up, blue eyes darkly lined, spaghetti-strap top, clingy short skirt, three-inch heels on her sandals. She had been clean for two months, though she looked cheap. Or is that just the way teenagers dress these days? I wondered.

Lila took us inside, introduced us to three or four girls shooting pool in the rec room. They each smiled and made eye contact with us.

Lila led us to a wrap-around veranda out front, lined with old Adirondack chairs. I embraced her, and when she pulled away, I noticed her small breasts, no bra, the short lycra skirt clinging to her crotch.

I sat for a while, with a book in my lap, staring at the large blue Maxwell House cans planted by every chair, filled with cigarette butts. A screen door slammed hard, and a woman I had not been introduced to in the rec room sat down a few chairs over.

"Would you like something to drink?" she asked with a faint Southern drawl.

"No thanks," I said, "I've just had a twenty-ounce Coke on the drive up."

"Oh, I love Coca-Cola about this time in the afternoon. Coke's my poison now, it's such a pick-me-up. We're all hooked on Cokes and cigarettes, you know."

I smiled.

"Where do you stay?" she asked.

"Oh, I'm on vacation, I'm not from here. I live in California."

"We've got ice cream and we're making coffee. Wouldn't you like something?" she insisted.

She reached over to put her cigarette out in the coffee can. Both forearms were covered with tattoos of gorgons and snakes. From a distance, they looked like long mesh gloves. Small spots of pale skin flashed through. She got up and walked back into the house without saying anything, leaving a sweet air of sweat and talc behind.

The screen door flew open again and again slammed shut. Two unfamiliar heavyset women in frayed cutoffs and bleached hair emerged and sat down farther away, picking up packs of cigarettes that had been left on a small teak table.

"Who you visiting?" one asked without looking at me.

"I came up with Lila's mother to keep her company."

"Oh. Where you from?"

"The West Coast. And you?"

"West Virginia. I'm a big girl from a small state," she laughed.

"I'm bigger than you are," said the other woman. "Sally's bigger than me," she giggled.

"Bigger is better," the girl from West Virginia said.

"You're putting it on here, you keep up with that gravy and you'll be bigger than me," the other woman laughed.

"You're gonna be big as that truck that drives by every day. Then I'm gonna paint a big sign on you saying, MAN WANTED."

The girl from West Virginia took a deep drag from her cigarette and looked out onto the highway.

"Looks like you can spot everyone who drives by," I said awkwardly.

"Yeah, it's just about time for that asshole to make his rounds. Every day I've been here, a man in a black pickup drives by with the words WOMAN WANTED painted on it. He looks out the window at us girls, drives slowly, but never gets out of the truck."

"Can you imagine?" one of the women turned to me.

"How desperate can you get?" the other said.

"He's worse off than we are."

Two dogs were tied up to a giant pine tree next door. The houses were separated by a wide, continuous lawn with no fence. A boy carrying a bag of groceries walked up the road, causing both dogs to bark furiously. The boy barked back, and kept walking, and disappeared from the view.

The women got up to go back into the house. I was alone for a few minutes, not really thinking about Lila, just staring at the row of empty chairs down the porch, the cool green of shade where the dogs lay down, now quiet. The humid heat felt like a companion with a mood.

A girl with liquid blue eyes wandered out of the house and said hello. She sat down in the next chair. Her skin was very clear and translucent, with no visible pores, no pierces.

"What are you reading?" she asked.

"It's a book by a French writer named Marcel Proust," I said, imagining she might not know who I was talking about. "It's a long book, in fact there are six or seven of them, his life's work."

"Oh, is it good?"

"Well, it's enough to keep you pretty busy on long trips," I said.

Her hair was soft and feathery, not teased like the other girls, no makeup.

She lit a cigarette.

"So," I asked, "what do you do around here on Saturday night?"

"We have meetings, we go to a lot of meetings every day, a little boring but necessary."

We looked out at the road, and beyond that a trailer park, with tall trees, figures moving, mostly hidden. The sound of a child's crying floated across the street in between cars. In the heat, one thing at a time seemed to appear, so that each discreet thing felt important.

She spoke softly, looking straight at me, flicking her cigarette but not looking down at it.

"How long have you been here?" I asked her.

"Oh, I'm leaving next week. Getting an apartment in town with another girl. I've been clean for six months."

"You have a job?"

"I'm trying for one. Babysitting four kids."

"That's tough work. Well maybe you can get them to babysit each other."

"I like kids. I like to be with them."

"Taking care of kids isn't for everybody. Parents are sort of paranoid and suspicious about people who stay with their kids. I mean," I fumbled, "it takes a particular kind of person."

"You got kids?"

"No, but I have a niece, she's almost nine."

"Oh, that's such a good age, they're so sweet at nine."

"Yes," I said, "so sweet."

She looked at me again, her unblemished face, her clear sad blue eyes.

"You have much contact with the men here?"

"Not really. Well, we see them at meetings. But it's discouraged, getting together with them, you're not even supposed to talk with them personally."

"Why's that?" I asked.

"It wouldn't be good. I mean, we're all so sick, I mean, what kind of relationship could you have?"

"OK, who wants a haircut?" Earlene, one of the women I'd met inside, stepped out onto the porch twirling a pair of hair scissors and a plastic spray bottle.

"Debbie's gonna get a haircut. Who else?"

"Oh, God, that's a big thing, I mean, I don't know if I'm ready," another said. "I need a cut but," she said, touching the ends of her hair, smoothing the sides.

"Just the ends," Debbie said, "just the damn ends."

A car drove by fast, its brakes screeched at the bend, and everybody looked out.

Earlene shook out a cloth and fitted it around Debbie's neck and chest and back to catch the hairs.

"You must be professional by the way you stuck that spray bottle into your pocket," I said.

"I am. I got my teacher's license last time I was incarcerated," she said. "I'm good."

She pulled out the bottle and sprayed Debbie's long hair and started to comb it out and do the usual hairdresser things, parting sections and putting them aside. She didn't have hair clips, so she twisted the hair and stuck it on top of Debbie's head, and it stayed twisted until she needed it.

When she got to the back of Debbie's head, she muttered something under her breath.

"What the fuck?" said Debbie. "What?"

"I said, is your hair uneven!"

"Whad'ya mean uneven? My mother paid sixty-five dollars for a fancy haircut for me and you're telling me it's uneven?"

"Well, whoever the fuck cut your hair for sixty-five dollars didn't know shit about cutting hair. She layered the fucking bottom, not the top, see."

Earlene held up chunks of hair to prove the ineptness of the previous stylist.

"Well, just take off the split ends, will you?"

"Well, do you want me to even it off or do you want to fucking go around with crooked hair?"

"For Chrissake, I don't want to go around with crooked hair. Even it out!" she commanded.

"And the bangs, don't forget the bangs, but not too short."

Earlene worked quietly, snipping the ends.

"Almost finished," she said.

"Wow," I said, "you're quick."

"Yeah, she's quick. She knows what she's doing. Those sixty-five-dollar cutters don't know jack shit, they just drag it out to make you think you're getting your money's worth."

Earlene called out to the girl with the clear blue eyes.

"So Erica, you want a trim?"

Erica touched the ends of her hair feathering her neck.

"Well, I need a trim, but I don't know. We gotta go to group in forty-five minutes."

By the time Mara and Lila returned, Erica's soft waves were falling onto the wooden floor of the porch. The electric shaver buzzed like an amplified mosquito. She flicked a hair from her cheek.

"Gadzooks, what are you doing?" Lila widened her eyes, and flipped her long black braid over her shoulder. She seemed excited from the brief furlough with her mother.

"She's getting a trim, honey," the haircutter laughed, "a close trim."

"Christ, you're gonna look like you're in basic training, Erica."

"Well, I am, I guess," Erica sighed.

Lila phoned Mara a few days after we visited. Mara wanted to mention art school, but Lila was still too trembly for the future.

"Glad you called before church, Mom."

"Church?" I heard Mara ask. She motioned for me to pick up the cordless phone in the bedroom.

"Hey, can Amy get on the extension? We can have a double date here."

"So good to see you guys," Lila squealed. "The girls liked you, Amy."

"Yeah, I talked to quite a few of them."

"Yeah. They don't get many visitors up here, just family and stuff. And some don't get that."

"Mmm, that's too bad. I mean, that their family doesn't come to visit."

"God, I hate it here. But what choice do I have?"

Lila refused to endorse what was happening to her, she just went along with it.

"I'm not like these girls. . . ."

"I'm sorry Lila," Mara said. "The doctor said you were doing so much better."

"When's Daddy coming up?"

"Next weekend?"

"I'm not like them. I'm not," she insisted. "I hate them, they don't talk to me, we don't have anything to talk about. The only thing we have in common is the air we breathe."

"Hey, you're forgetting something," Mara said.

"Yeah, I'm forgetting something. Yeah, we're all sick, that's what we have in common. We're all addicts."

Mara fell silent, and nothing came out of my mouth, either. The word had a life we couldn't recognize.

"I asked them what you were talking about," Lila said brightly. "You know with Erica and Earlene and stuff? They told me just stuff, confidential stuff. They said they 'weren't no snitches.' I should ask you if I wanted to know. They're big into confidential here."

Kafka's Bride

H'S IS A SMALL story in a large sky. There is always a book under her arm. H died of history but stayed young forever. H herself is a small story in a large book. H found Kafka, and speaks to me from heaven, so I can speak for her. Last time she spoke, she said, *Keep watch over absent meaning.* I am sure she read this in a book. H is reunited with sisters A and G and brother B, of course. G and A and B, who died old and estranged, blame the marriages they made, it being a little too late to influence events anymore, theirs being other small stories in a large sky, but Kafka is the only one not justifying or judging stories retroactively all wrong in advance. Kafka knows of unretractable destruction. But H is fresh, full of vitality, eager, and always about to be sexual. She strides down the stone street, the Polish light catching her stylish bob, a beret over one ear, a tailored jacket belted around her tiny waist, a straight skirt with side pleats, wedgies and little white socks. There is a book under her arm, but we cannot read the title. There is a Star of David sewn to her sleeve. She is always just come from school. H knew the outcome of this marriage G and A concocted for B and C. C isn't there yet, just so you know. I don't think C will ever get there. Having died first, H had special privileges. The gift of early death is to be able to know the future of those you love but not to be able to do anything about it. Like a pier burned in the middle, history drops off and begins again. Truly, the preacher said, it didn't matter which question you failed to answer, how you perished, you'd soon be able to review the whole thing, old war buddies having a beer and naming the exact parallel in a foreign country where other buddies went down, or exploits in the trenches, etc. The average life expectancy at Auschwitz was five weeks. H is one question in a book of eternal symptoms, H is effect in a narrative of causes. Heaven is a card game where old women with tinted hair talk of mitzvahs without lifting their eyes from the cards. The laughter of children is the only music in heaven. You die and you remain that age forever, and you are free of history, but you know the future. H died with a book under her arm, and though the title is faded, the book remains. H could see the atomic bomb clear as print. There was no question of looking away. Imagine what else she could see, the pages of the book burnt, the letters indestructible. But H is forever a young girl full of promise.

The world is full of hope but not for us, Kafka keeps whispering in her ear, but she ignores this aspect of him.

I return to the text to continue the conversations with my ancestors, she reminds him. Something else she read in a book. He's impressed. When they met, H loved him all the more for knowing her without her having to ask. Perhaps the book she carries on her way home from school was written by him. She could fit herself into the generality of history, knowing how deeply he felt in the particular. Hers is a small story in a large sky. He accepts her as his only bride.

Live Oak

I WAS SITTING in the park under that old wisteria tree. The one that gives off sublime white blossoms for a couple of weeks in the spring.

Stray petals stuck to the nap of my black sweater. I absently stuck a Kleenex into the back pages of a book I'd just begun. The weather was mild and across the lawn, a young woman sat in a folding chair, her waist-length hair fanned out to her shoulders. Next to the play area, the usual pickup basketball, tall dark men in their tank tops, grunting, their sweaty chests pumped up and poised like statues for the next jump shot.

In the sandbox, a little girl held up her red plastic binoculars in order to spy on a boy high up the climbing structure. The sun struck a metal buckle on his overalls, and for a moment he was the Star of Bethlehem atop the crazy geometry.

The man who took up nightly residence on the bench against the cinder-block recreation center hadn't quite situated himself behind his tableaux of carts stuffed with collages and paperbacks and old radios with their cords dangling out. Purses and small duffel bags swung from the rusted metal grates. The women inside the rec center would be sweating and clapping to their six o'clock Jazzercise beat. *That's the way, uh-huh uh-huh, we like it, uh-huh uh-*

huh, that's the way, uh-uh uh-huh, we like it. . . . He'd try to get a little reading in before dark.

The gate to the tot swings creaked as a young mother tried to flip the latch and maneuver a stroller and a big diaper bag and twin boy toddlers tugging at her purse.

"Lady," a homeless woman approached me, and I knew, anyone knows what's coming next. She was both old and young and wiry and full, her smile soft and open on a deeply crinkled, handsome face. She wore layers of clothes above her bare feet. A red bandanna jaunty around her neck. A wooden cross on a leather thong.

There's an encampment, invisible by day, just below the bridge, by the creek and the picnic tables, under the redwoods and giant live oaks. When the sun goes down, there's a village with no name where people gather and trade their wares and speak and eat and wash their clothes and make love and sigh and sleep.

All the things anyone does inside.

"Lady," she said again, as she moved closer, still smiling. Our eyes met, she looked me up and down, and then she turned away.

"What?" I shouted after her.

It's a law of nature, at least my nature, to answer someone who approaches me with goodwill and suddenly backs off. There's the unfinished business, hanging in midair like a sentence without a period.

I got up from my pleasant spot beneath the fragrant blossoms and followed her across the wet lawn.

She moved fast toward the creek, her feet almost gliding above the grass, and I had to run a little.

"What did you want back there?" I caught up with her. "Did you need something?"

We stood face to face. She looked at me, no smile now. We were the same height and similar build. She seemed younger than on first impression, she seemed my age.

"What makes you think I wanted anything from you?"

"Well, you called out to me. You. . . ."

"Well, I changed my mind. I have everything I want."

"What made you change your mind?"

I don't know why I pressed her, I don't know why I needed to know.

"Are you hungry?" I asked.

"Why are you harassing me, lady?"

"You said, 'Lady,' back there . . . you must have wanted some money or something."

"This is preposterous," she said. "A person can't stroll around a public park without getting hit up, a person can't go about their own business without disturbing the social order. What's wrong with you?"

"I, I. . . ." The wind picked up and the pollens whirled and I began to sneeze. One sneeze after another. Tears formed in the corners of my eyes.

She stared at me, but I could hardly see her.

"Why don't you mind your own business?" she said.

I took a Kleenex out of my pocket to wipe my eyes and blow my nose.

"Didn't anyone ever tell you not to talk to strangers?" she said softly. "Why don't you take care of yourself? Why don't you go home where you belong?"

Love

A WOMAN FELL in love with a butcher. It seems unlikely, to fall in love with a man with blood on his hands, I mean, for a grown though admittedly shy woman to actively fall in love with a butcher man who is a grown man, not a butcher in training, not a man who you've already fallen in love with and who decides later that butchering is a good job that pays well and from which you are unlikely to be laid off, these being such uncertain times, that is, of course, unless the country turns vegetarian, which is improbable. It would be hard to fall in love with a mortician, say, seeing as it would probably be love at first and last sight. I mean, how often would you, if you were a shy person, have cause to cross a mortician's path so as to get to know him?

But this butcher, he was incredible to look at, which is why the woman fell in love with him. That sort of love — and of course, women are not exempt from it. It is not credible or artful to say that she fell in love with him after she'd asked for eight, exactly eight sausages and after he asked her, "Would there be anything else?" There was nothing at all phallic about their transaction, despite the nature of the exchange, he handing her the wrapped sausages and all, just after he'd picked each one off the tray, placed them carefully on the paper spread across the cup of his hand, folded up the package on the counter, taped it up, and written on the white wrapping paper. Or did he slap one of those computer-ized tags across the folds? I can't remember what she said, I can only recall her recounting that no money passed between them.

The woman, grown as she was, was rusty at love, but love conquers all, even puts words into the mouths of the mute, thoughts into the heads of the stupid, doubt into the minds of the smug. It makes accountants artistic and gives lawyers belief in the unseen. What does it do to butchers, who after all, have every opportunity on earth to flirt with thousands of women a week? It causes butchers to add a ninth sausage to an order of eight.

A butcher is, after all, a worker of the world, not necessarily without refinement, though perhaps more likely to demonstrate a certain, shall we say, earthbound generosity. It is not as though his personal spirits cannot soar, no. But among the professions not likely to enjoy unification, among all the artist-massage therapists, actor-waiters, screenwriter-plumbers, dancer-nurses . . . in the world of hyphenated identities springing up like a sort of bi-occu-pationalism, never have we encountered a poet-butcher.

This is perhaps sad.

His face, something like Gregory Peck crossed with Cary Grant, his eyes, somewhat like Omar Sharif crossed with Sidney Poitier, was deputed by fate to appear behind the meat counter of a supermar-ket, and this grown woman, well, she leaned heavily against the glass, her tongue tied in the usual places, and at last rather rudely, without an "excuse me" or anything, waited for him to wrap her order. Her abruptness sprung from cold fear. She murmured:

"Were you something else before you became a butcher?"

She was certain he had another life, a previous vocation, at the very least some other position that might make use of his dashing, soulful features. Or was her inquiry simply a way of beginning a dialogue?

Tell all the truth but tell it slant, success in circuit lies.

This famous admonition by the poet Emily Dickinson was not in her mind as she spoke. However, years of training as a female, though out of practice since she had long ceded most of the antique etiquette of her sex, and it all came back to her. To be coy as one is aggressive. This took art. What better way to approach an extremely handsome man but by asking *him* about him?

"Well, I I I. . . ."

He was, needless to say, petrified. Her forwardness, her leaning into the counter that contained the vastest variety of sausages West of the Mississippi, perhaps West of Mars—Burmese Curry, Chicken Apple, Smoked Lemon Chicken, Turkey Anise Cilantro, Rosemary Basil Duck, Smoked Whiskey Fennel, and the modest though arguably more mysterious, Italian, not to mention the enigmatic though perhaps more suspect, Chorizo. None of which is relevant to our account here.

And she fell madly in love. And this love gave her confidence to open her eyes as widely as God allows shy women to open their eyes, and wait for his reply.

"Well, I ah I used to play ball, but then I was injured. . . ."

"Oh," she said. "Major leagues?"

An extremely gauche thing to ask, for if she at all knew what she was talking about she would have said, "Majors."

"Nah, didn't get that far. . . ."

This grown woman smiled. It had been a long, extremely dry year since the emotion behind the smile could at all be offered or interpreted as sincere.

"Well," she blurted out, "you look like a . . . soap opera actor, a. . . ."

And here she corrected herself, for who knows what image of daytime television a butcher of the night shift held dear. . . .

"You look like a matinée idol."

"Well, uh, thank you," he said wiping his hands on his apron and turning to the next customer.

She knew, that is, knew in the corporeal sense, nothing about butchers, bakers, candlestick-makers, shoemakers, soap opera actors, matinée idols or idolaters, and least of all did she know anything about playing ball, which presumably though perhaps falsely may have been baseball, as opposed to any other kind of ball he may have played and been, poor thing, injured by. Perhaps her question was even stupider than she imagined, for perhaps he had played football, but of course, there were those large warm eyes, and he was not a large man, not even a Joe Montana, nor did his shoulders reveal any other bulk besides the normal sort accrued by lifting legs and loins.

As though she knew anything about that.

She wanted to tell this butcher that he was the handsomest man in the place (this place being a supermarket, where once a famous and great poet had asked why he could not buy what he needed with his good looks, and she had a similar thought, why on earth such a good-looking man even had to work for a living). She wanted to know what he thought of her, of nuclear testing, of private property, of public education; she wanted to be smart aleck and clever and yell out, "Hey good-looking!" the way a smart-alecky man might have and may still do to women in other places on earth, without being taken for a jerk. God, she wanted to say, "You are so handsome. You are so unbelievable, why are you a butcher, I mean, why?"

But instead, there arose in her . . . hopeless, already thwarted desires. For how, after all these years, could she bring home a butcher? Her grandmother, who'd buried four husbands, married a butcher during the Depression, a precise calculation that yielded the appropriate results. The family ate well during the leanest of years. But does ontogeny always recapitulate phylogeny?

Then of course other tropes appeared from the interceding decades, such as The Butcher of Lyon. It seemed indecent to love a man who spent all day dressing flesh in a corner of a market. It was not possible to imagine offspring who when asked what their father did would reply, "Butcher."

It is for this reason, and I let you in on this secret, for it is an important though overlooked principle, that life is far more implausible than art, that having heard this story, having witnessed the full range of emotion slide across this grown woman's face, octaves of dormant desire pinged into life by a chance encounter with a butcher, that because of his utter butcherness and the highly likely probability that you as reader might be grossed out by the thought of a love affair with a man who had blood on his hands, that I cannot in all modesty continue this tale of the grown woman and the aforesaid handsome man, without changing his vocation to something less carnal, more contemporary, more plausible, more palatable, such as clerk or physicist or priest or professor.

So the story begins:

A woman fell in love with a nightclub hypnotist. . . .

The Oldest Trick in the Book

for love all love of other sights controls
    —John Donne

WHEN A PLACE seems worn out—when everything's dusty and there's only one horse to get to the other end of town on and it's lame—the oldest trick in the book is to show it to someone new.

This works especially well if the possibility of romance sits on the horizon like a wall of rain.

And if one party in the proverbial twosome holds himself tight as a corset, another party must accept the challenge.

He knocked at the door, right on time, come from a fairly long distance, immediately started in about someone he knew who would take the house off my hands. I was vaguely thinking of selling, trying to get out of town, though I felt slow about it, alone and unsure of where to begin. I could see him working hard to offset his corset problem, standing in the entryway, talking fast. So the only thing to do was show him around, even upstairs where the bedrooms were.

You know, I'm not the kind of woman accustomed to showing men where the bedrooms are, but in the spirit of a possible sale, I did. After all, why should a vulturous pimp called a real estate agent make money off my contempt for private property?

Of course, I would have rather reserved this poignant tour for after the date, offering him the solace of a good night's sleep in one of the many empty beds.

Not mine, of course, since that would be the quickest way to get this particular man out the door. I thought.

So we toured the house, and then decided upon a nearby restaurant and that we would walk there, and later downtown, for a movie, this being a day date.

He was a cautious, gentle man who didn't want to succumb to the night and its usual temptations. I already was dark as night and that was frightening enough for him.

It was my town, had been mine for too many years, through children, husbands, and a fair piece of a declining century, and like a lot of other college towns, Berkeley was once small, livable, stimulating and cranky and sylvan but always safe and negotiable. It had lost the last two features over a short period of time, and now a whole generation couldn't remember when there weren't armed muggings, impossible traffic congestion. Just the other day, my best friend told me that her neighbors went out for an evening walk and got robbed at gunpoint by three guys who pulled up alongside them in a Volvo.

Then there were the homeless. And these bore no resemblance to the hippies of a former era. These were the bona fide lost, whose lost time had come, many of whose mental flowers had wilted right on their vines. Before Reaganomics threw acid in our eyes, we certainly had never seen a tiny rag of a child holding out a hand outside a market except if we crossed the international border to the south.

At one time, Berkeley had a foreign policy. Not that I'm an isolationist, but don't these things begin *chez nous*?

"Oh is this the famous Chez Panisse?" he exclaimed as we walked down Shattuck Avenue past Vine Street. The steps to this modest establishment were right at the sidewalk, and he drew back as if in awe of its reputation.

"Yes," I said. We gazed at the menu, he seemed interested, so I led him inside. He followed behind, unsure, and I, who rarely march into places I don't frequent, strode with a confidence that could only be attributed to his presence.

There was a hint of piñon smoke in the air. A monumental bouquet of white lilies and *matilija* poppies, with their papery petals and egg-yolk centers, graced a small reception table at the base of the stairs. We peeked inside the dining room, which at this time was empty. We ascended the stairs to the café, and in the soft low lights and woody intimacy, diners lingered at white linen tablecloths finishing their last sauternes. We approached the bar, examined the lunch menu, goat cheese arugula salads, elaborate tarts with names of olives we couldn't pronounce, and haughtily decided not.

The sun uncharacteristically bore down on us as we strolled south along Shattuck, after a leisurely lunch of cheap Thai food, and we cut over to Oxford somewhere near campus. There was a bustle of construction work and street traffic and bicycles flitting by. School had just begun and the town had the faint hum of bees about to descend somewhere nearby.

Did I know where I was taking him? Not really, as in the many years of my tenure in Berkeley, I had never actually used the route we were walking but somehow with him I trusted that directionals wouldn't fail. We talked as we walked by the Theater Department, by Dwinelle Hall, then entered the cool interiors of the Morrison Room at Doe Library, with its elegant autumnal light, tightly upholstered settees, and vast Persian rugs.

I pointed out special collections of poetry which perhaps

impressed him more than it ought to have since he assumed that I actually frequented this place more than I did. I wanted him and so I wanted to revive the charm of a town I had long since grown disenchanted with. Could these beautiful places compensate for the dusty worn-out feeling, the demise of rent control, the proliferation of chain stores, the growing menace of guns and knives, the private miseries that were regularly perched on the streets like not so invisible weapons?

Perhaps not, but as we ambled through campus, even hurried down Telegraph Avenue for a couple of chaotic blocks, a thoroughly refreshing effect had occurred—his eyes had suddenly become mine.

In the theater, he bought a large Coke, I grabbed two straws and plunged them into the plastic cup cover, and he laughed, not imagining it possible. The movie was poor and we sat in our separate seats quite separately. He was still, I squirmed and shifted my legs and arms and no position seemed comfortable. The air-conditioning got colder, I reached for my jacket and coins dropped onto the floor, and I nearly knocked over the soda. I kept waiting for him to take one of my useless hands and hold it as I remembered boys always did with girls a long time ago.

But the gesture was withheld, even outmoded at our age, and a strange resolve to avoid physical contact veiled a certain heat just underneath the resolve.

We emerged from the theater into the glare of early evening, and as it was late summer, the sun seemed to collide with the moon and they both cast a dramatic light on the marquee. Not bright enough for sunglasses, a few blinks away from dusk. We stood in front of the building. I was hungry but assumed he wanted to head back to my house so that he could embark upon the long drive to his.

"I'm hungry," I announced with impunity and certainly without any motive of detaining him.

"I could eat a little," he rejoined.

I suggested we walk in the direction of a nearby Moroccan restaurant.

The owner waltzed outside the moment we arrived, as though on the lookout for customers. His extraordinary green eyes met mine and I thought he might remember me from a previous dinner. He behaved as though he did remember, moved close to me with an ardent, erotic air.

He escorted us to a table in the back, past the banquette, the small inlaid brass tables and low backless stools with cushions, Middle Eastern style, where one's knees inconveniently could not support spines as old as ours. There was a small stage against the front window framed by palm fronds and a sign that advertised belly dancers and music.

"You haven't got a wine license yet?" I asked, leaning into the waiter's handsome countenance.

"Oh no," he demurred. "We have good beer, though. And there's a liquor store across the street, you can bring in anything you like."

"Oh, beer, I . . ." and I was not in the mood for interrupting the mood my companion and I were in, the tentative prolongation of an afternoon, albeit not *sur l'herbe*, still, one graced with a salutary replacement of bad attitude. Suddenly Berkeley began to look lovely to me, as though it might be a place I'd like to visit.

"Well, I do," the waiter said, in a perfectly modulated *sotto voce*, "have my own personal bottle of wine in the refrigerator, which I could sell you for ten dollars. . . ."

"Ah," I said, "oh that would be wonderful."

I asked my companion if he would share the bottle with me.

He hemmed and hawed and muttered something about beer, intimated the drive home, but in the end we shared the bottle, a modest adequate chardonnay.

The spirits did their work, and soon the dis-ease that permeated the afternoon, the restraint around the edges, the veneer of sadness I had begun to feel but would rather die than express directly, evaporated from me.

I paid for dinner and we cut across Shattuck at Berkeley Way to walk along Milvia.

"Well, the music was pretty impressive in that movie, don't you think?"

"Mmm," I agreed. I was being silent. I was being strange with myself, not wanting him to say the inevitable, and when he mentioned that he'd get home not too late, our eyes met, my throat constricted, and he instantly sensed my sadness at his impending departure.

Was it guilt that arose in him? Who can say? Who can say if I played that guilt or whether the wine had unmoored me sufficiently to state the obvious?

"The movie wasn't good enough," I said.

"Mmm?" he said.

"I mean, the movie wasn't good enough to prevent me from wanting to kiss you."

This was precisely how I'd felt, except that I'd felt even more. I'd felt that I wanted him to rip my blouse off, there during that rather mediocre cinematic experience. For what else can a darkened room serve on a brilliant sunny day but as refuge for the desirous?

And of course language produced the desired results.

We kissed in the middle of the sidewalk, and kept kissing until at last he became embarrassed and suggested a deeper side street.

Now it was me who took hold of his hand and led him up the path, though not without a certain awkwardness. Our hips were exactly equal in height, parallel, a phenomenon I had never experienced with another person. They bumped up against one another and so he let go my hand and put his arm around my waist. This too proved an unsatisfactory means of locomotion, as we came upon the dimly lit exterior of the Church of the Magdalen on upper Milvia.

I led him to the bench in front of the chapel. We sat for a few moments and kissed again, but again he seemed deeply uncomfortable and wanted to resume the kissing at my house.

"Shall we take the high road to the house by the rushing stream," I asked, "or the low road through the park?" The question appeared rhetorical until he said, "The low road."

We walked along the bridge where Strawberry Creek narrows. "It's rushing here too," he said.

Only we could not hear it as we could have across the street. I was conscious of the homeless encampment in the dark under the tall fir trees a few hundred feet from the bridge.

I led him across the wet grass and up the hill to my house.

We stood at the door and kissed some more. There was talk of his leaving, there was talk of his staying. I reminded him of the vacant beds upstairs, and he was quick to say that if he stayed, he would stay in my bed, with me.

I had little desire for him to stay, having secured what I did desire, but I left the decision up to him.

We were thirsty, on account of the sound of the rushing stream still in our ears, on account of the wine and the warm balm of the evening.

He did not like ice in his water. We took the bottle and sat on the back porch, close but not touching, and he reviewed the other evenings we had spent together, feeling at last the emotional platform he evidently needed to stand on so that his profound reticence might recede.

He left in the morning. The town took on a cast it had for so long forfeited in my eyes, over the years of the demise of its infrastructure. It was as though someone were watching my movements, my most ordinary movements, as I held the key to the door of the car and unlocked the lock and slid into the driver's seat.

Homologue

ON A PLANE FLIGHT from San Francisco to New York, I remembered that my uncle was dead.

Though he'd been dead for years, his absence was not real to me. He had had a great affection for me, and he had been in love with New York. Perhaps because of this happy conjunction, I went out of my way to spend time with him whenever I could. He was synonymous with New York, and like many veteran New Yorkers, he extolled the virtues of Manhattan and endured certain material deprivations and stresses as if they were privileges.

New Yawkk is like living in all places on earth at once, he insisted, after a brisk walk from Chelsea to the Guggenheim, which by California standards constitutes a hike. We would take long morning coffees at the breakfast table after my aunt had left for work. We would speak of the latest art, of foreign policy, of wars I barely followed, and he would eat slice after slice of buttered rye toast, his pale blue eyes twinkling with the impish knowledge that he was transgressing doctor's orders. His heart was always open and bursting. He was equally enthusiastic about the day ahead, a new diva at the Met, a tree in bloom, a recent Supreme Court hearing, and he did not count calories. He was a man who liked to joke that he left Russia in a potato sack to flee the Bolsheviks, only to become a Communist in America.

Everyone cherished him, even his children, and no one, besides me, dressed in black for his funeral. My aunt wore a shiny, emerald green shift, no hosiery. Perhaps I had lived in Berkeley too long, where dark-to-black attire ruled any important occasion. No adult I knew wore shiny green, let alone short and tight.

"Your mom looks great in that outfit," I whispered to my cousin at the wake.

"Oh," she smiled. "Max would have liked it that way, so he could see her legs."

As a young person, I felt I knew Max well enough and assumed, as the young naturally assume, that he would live alongside of all that mattered to me as long as I did. And then suddenly he died one evening, slumped over the toilet, next to a book titled *Beyond God*.

When we remember someone we love and who loved us, we remember their gestures, their actions, their sound, their smell. *Faint tea, witch hazel diluted in rose water, Old Spice. Cream and three cubes of sugar, a stained necktie, Cezanne is my man, you'll come to Mozart, you'll see. Taxi, taxi, we are three, wheeee. . . .* Like children, we cannot remember them inanimate or not there. *Why do you cry when a man reads to you, you don't cry when Max reads to you? Max is different, he's not a man, he's Max.* And unless we have literally found them mute and stiff to our pleas, or gazed at their waxen likeness resting in a ruffled satin they never knew alive, we do not remember them dead.

My uncle's death was foretold by a man who died ten months before him. That man was my father, his brother-in-law.

One of the last times I saw my father was with my uncle. He was as different from my uncle as a smile is from a scream. After my uncle left the house, I found my father crying in a dark hallway.

"Daddy," I said, in a voice that belonged to a child, the distinct soprano of a six-year-old. I was a grownup with children of my own, and I had never seen my father depart from the even-tempered, uneventful demeanor I knew him by and expected of him.

"Daddy," I repeated. "What's wrong, why are you crying?"

For all the years I knew him, my father consistently offered an exterior that did not reveal the anguish he kept from himself. This moment, in which I was suddenly privy to the hidden, was shocking to me.

"Because, because," he sobbed. "Max looks so old and I know I'll never see him again. It's happened so fast! My life!"

It was not until long after my father's death that I would gather obvious clues to the sorrows he kept closely guarded within himself. His dying, unlike my uncle's, created a much deeper portrait of him, a portrait once denied to me by our respective roles. Thus my father's death, his physical absence from my life, appears quite real to me, as pieces of him reveal themselves in time, and seem to plot a fascinating series of actions and their consequences, of which I am and am not a part.

For a child, a father's life also happens quite fast, perhaps as fast as my father himself lamented. A large piece of a father's life is unknown to a child, the most important piece, that is, the life of the man before the life of the father.

It was not until my father's death that I discovered his passport, a worn document that charted the countries he had visited long before my birth. Folded inside the center of the little book was his first work permit, with a photograph of him as a boy. His hair was wavy and his eyes distant, like a young Rimbaud. An old social security card, the red numbers faded to pink, and a yellowed slip of paper fluttered to the floor. Printed in pencil, not in his handwriting, were the words, BERSTEIN'S MILL. <u>Friday</u>.

While the father lives, it is inconceivable to the child that the most important things in a parent's life may have occurred before the child was born. And that the child should grow up in the aura of gone events that surrounded the father like the enigmatic, glowing rings of Saturn. And yet these inconceivable proceedings enter the child and become part of the child's imagination, as surely as any coeval events.

Shortly after the War, Max, an unemployed student, entered the lobby of the Flatiron Building in Manhattan and walked up several fights of stairs to visit his brother-in-law Harry. Harry rented an eighth-floor loft where he manufactured women's lingerie. Max needed to borrow money from Harry. The elevator was broken that day.

Instead of greeting his brother-in-law, Harry immediately handed him a large shopping bag stuffed with scraps of cloth.

"Take this out of here, keep it for me, and I'll call you later," Harry instructed Max. "Someone's coming. Leave now," he demanded.

Harry was a man of spare language, never prone to adjectives or otherwise embellishing his remarks. His form of hyperbole was always manifest in action or the few ostentatious objects he purchased for his home. He was a quiet, small man who chose massive red velvet curtains for the living room and a plush gold-colored sofa with matching armchairs. These decisions were his, not his wife's, as she had no mind for such matters.

Max was surprised, yet obeyed his brother-in-law. They were close in age but each thought the other was a fool. Marriage and family had brought two men together whose paths might never have crossed otherwise. They were born in a geography whose borders shifted according to the caprices of war. Both spoke dialects of the same language, both lost their fathers in early childhood. One fled the twin persecutions of the cossacks and then the Bolsheviks, and the other, the infernos of the Nazis.

The bag was heavy. Climbing down the back stairs of the strange angular building and believing himself to be alone, Max sat down on a landing to investigate the bulging bag of fabric scraps. It was filled instead with money, not the neat orderly stacks of bills featured in gangster movies which seem to fit perfectly in black attaché cases that reveal their contents abruptly after the locks click open, but paper money of all denominations—some crumpled, some flat, some folded, some rolled and fastened with rubber bands.

Frightened, perhaps more of the condition of the cash, rather than the money itself, Max ran to the nearest subway entrance and nervously boarded a train that would take him to his sister's house.

He might have boarded a train for Coney Island and strolled the deserted boardwalk where the wind from the winter ocean would have forced him to hold the shopping bag between his legs while he buttoned his overcoat. Or he might have taken the El for Boropark, where he would feel protected by thick swarms of Jewish kinsmen in long black frock coats and curly locks framing their bearded faces. He might have hopped a bus for the Frick Museum where he would fearfully fumble with the shopping bag, attempting to disguise it, stuff it into his coat, or simply check it, then stroll among the Persian rugs and giant Fragonards amassed by a robber baron. He could have easily slipped into a nearby automat, where he would casually sit down to a watery cup of coffee, clutch the shopping bag close to his overcoat, watch the tired and the poor line up for the blue plate specials, and wait for night-fall. Or he might have gone on foot to the New York Public Library, where he could quickly ascend the front steps guarded by those stone lions, Patience and Fortitude, find a seat in the cavernous reading room at a long oak table, and leisurely turn the pages of a large book filled with beautiful reproductions of early Turners. He might have taken the long ride to the Cloisters, in Fort Tryon Park, and roamed in the liturgical air.

He could have gone anywhere, but I do not know where that was.

When my uncle told me fragments of this story, it revealed much about him. I was too young to ask for the missing pieces, perhaps too surprised. I did not wonder for a moment, at least not until this moment, how such immense temptation might have affected him.

He had recently returned from the European front, wounded in battle, and as yet without work. He enrolled in City College to study art history, and handed over most of his monthly GI bill to my grandmother, who was husbandless and poor.

During the war, my father had been engaged in certain activities that later in my life would contribute to our flight from New York to California, certain unsavory if not illegal business transactions. I do not know the exact nature of these transactions, for they originated in a foreign place at an equally foreign time before my birth, and yet they partly determined my destiny.

A small but revealing homologue here will suffice. On one of the few occasions when my brother visited me, long after we had both left home, he arrived at my doorstep, in a city unknown to him, with a paper bag full of clothes that he had apparently thrown together in haste. At the time, I made no comment to him. Later, sitting on the bed, I watched him rummage through several pairs of underwear and pull out a series of crumpled hundred-dollar bills, followed by wads of twenties and thick folds of singles held together by rubber bands. A rubber band snapped, the bills scattered across the bed. He scooped them up and stuffed them back into the sack. For the several days he stayed in my house, I eyed the shopping bag from the distance of the hall. It gave off an invisible radiating alarm. I couldn't bring myself to approach it even though it magnetized me.

There was always a partial grin on my uncle's face and a partial grimace on my father's. There was no look at all on my brother's face, as though he was unable to decide which look to offer the world. Or his face, defying history, independently determined not to express the condition of the rest of him. Should there be a look on his face, it might be one of self-contempt and its by-product, self-absorption.

My own countenance is largely unknown to me.

Rosie Since Vietnam

SHE'D BE LEAVING BERKELEY soon, she announced, and I said it was the same as if she'd said she had a terminal disease.

That's callow, I know, but when lives have mingled and accreted for as long as ours have, when there's only one other person in the world who can testify to your own tricky memory of your so-called self, well, you can't replace that. Gone from sight is gone.

"Listen," she said. "This isn't news. You could see it coming seven ways to Sunday."

Oh sure. I know. The spirit lives on. That's what she'd say, only she wouldn't say it clichéd. And anyway, she didn't liken her imminent departure to impending death. I did.

She tried to ease me into it, said she'd be gone south for the winter, so to speak. Only it was going to be for all the winters and all the summers for the rest of our lives. And we weren't that young anymore. And how many best friends do you make in a lifetime?

I was feeling sorry for myself in advance. Something like preoperative depression, if the metaphor holds. Loss was on the horizon, instead of the usual retrospective show I'm prone to trot out. I can be a regular curator then, trying to fit the many pieces of old grief side by side and think something new about them.

But as my son learned in a literary theory class last year, it could be time to kill off the grand narratives.

I resolved to get used to the idea of Rosie leaving before she departed.

She was fed up with her life in California and one of her kids went back to the South to college and her job got lousy with no benefits and a new nosey boss who wanted to join her for lunch once too many times, and there were no men she wanted except one whose terms were as lousy as the low-paying job and whose part-time romancing wasn't enough to sustain anybody older than a teenager.

It was like her love life was all benefits and no salary and that's an unsteady diet of ice cream and cake. A healthy grown woman generally craves more.

You keep thinking when a close friend says she's moving far away that you could have been a better friend, done something to make things easier, more fun, more beckoning. Things could be worse, I thought, I could have lost her to a guru. But that's folly, of course, because most everything anybody does has got its own reasons which you never saw while they were brewing right there under that person's skin. You can't predict. The more you know a person, the stranger they seem. You can't even prevent a suicide from her very own final solution.

She would be packing up like she did a couple times before, moving to a new town, new friends, this time, she said, not storing anything, not promising, just throwing out the old clothes, the soggy couch on the sidewalk, the stuff of her life a free-box for anyone else to scavenge.

"Darlin'," she would say to me every time she thought about moving, "darlin', we'll always be true-blue, won't we?" I took "always" as seriously as if it were written in my high school year-book.

Don't misunderstand. I don't blame her for wanting out of the hard mean drive-by life of the city. I don't blame her for wanting to go home to mythical Dixie. And I surely can't blame a woman who feels low on prospects and high on hope. And a beautiful woman who can go anywhere and be loved.

Not that a person's looks are any good reason to be friends with them, but she was a stunner. Hers was a beauty that for over twenty years never failed to make my pulse stop for just that tiny moment when you see someone you know well but haven't seen in a while and something in their countenance startles you brand new each time.

She could start all over anywhere because she generally got along talking to anybody and anything that would or wouldn't listen. People liked her because her big-eyed smile put them at ease and of course her grace — that irresistible magnet. She'd walk into a room not knowing anyone and never look sullen or bewildered or coy. She was persistent, she never stood on ceremony and she'd keep calling you until she got you live, and never complain that your line was busy or you didn't call her.

Her personality made for a meteoric rise at Sun & Moon Technologies, the company we once both worked for. S & M was an outfit that promised everything. We didn't go to school to work in computers, we fell into them. By the time we were thirty, we were old stories — married, kids, divorced, and both of us on welfare. There was a point when we said to one another, our lives are passing and we're not going with them. An ancient college degree wasn't worth much in most quarters anymore, but the computer industry seemed the last outpost of democracy. It took in Russian immigrants, ex-teachers, middle-aged men with record-breaking Beatles memorabilia, struggling poets, brilliant anarchists, your tired, your oppressed, your best girls turned women. And it took us. We wound up working for corporations that boomed and busted, handed out stock like candy, gave away products, threw expensive picnics with gourmet sausages, and then, as they say, bottom lined, bottomed out, and painfully padlocked their business park doors. At one time, we both worked for a place that had five layoffs in two years, till the employee population dwindled to the owners who had started the company in their garage.

Just before she was laid off S & M, Rosie got promoted to the head of marketing. Of course, by then she had no employees to direct, she was the only person in the department. I'd call her there, while I was licking the wounds of rejection before I found another job, and I'd always ask the receptionist who I got to be chummy with, and who they'd have to lay off last, "Please connect me to the Czarina of Marketing."

You've got to have a good sense of humor not to feel some kind of survivor's guilt when you've still got a job and your oldest friend doesn't.

But Rosie was not a guilty person and because she was free of this ordinary human misery, she was not a person to make you feel guilty.

She was a person to make you feel like you could go on, no matter what. That the world would take you in and you would fit. And that if you persisted, everything would work out.

There are times when I've thought happiness is just metabolic, you're born cheerful or you're born brooding and there is no more help for your disposition than there is for the color of your eyes.

Once, during the heyday of Sun & Moon, flush with expense accounts and sleek with two new very-marked-down suits from Saks, we flew to Japan on business. We were thrilled with the chance, in spite of the complicated child care arrangements. Did we have men in our lives then? I can't remember. A few days into our stay, we ventured out on our own with a map of Tokyo and a tiny tourist's dictionary. We were looking for the *ikebana*, the flower-arranging school, which was supposed to be not far from our hotel. We walked a ways, feeling pleasantly disoriented. Traffic flowed in reverse of what we were used to, and there weren't any street signs. At least none we could recognize. Green-and-white buses fluttered by like large silent toys, masses of noiseless people floated across large crosswalks. We got hungry, we turned up a small street lined with noodle parlors. A waitress scurried out of a shop, as we pointed at an elaborate display of plastic models of food in the window.

When we finished lunch, we strutted down the street, proud of having negotiated our first meal without company translators. Every few feet there were vending machines. I remember how thirsty we both got from the fish and seaweed, and how we would stop, deposit our yen, and watch the tiny cans of orange drink with lovely blue lettering drop to the window slot.

We were lost and of course we could easily have taken a taxi back to the hotel. But Rosie was, as I said, persistent, sure of her sense of direction and her will to succeed. We opened the map and stood in the middle of the sidewalk pondering it. Several pedestrians stopped and commiserated with us.

"We Arrrre Herrre," she put her finger on an abstract intersection in Tokyo. "Can you tell us, pleeese, how do we get to the School of Icky Baaanaaa?" She pointed and enunciated in a louder than usual English. And she smiled, even though she was very serious.

Each person who stopped would obediently lower his head to look closely at the map and then suck his breath in.

Once a passerby stopped, he stayed, feeling it a breach of international diplomacy to walk away. A crowd formed around us. We unfolded the entire map; perfect strangers held the four corners erect as though ready to catch a jumper from a burning building. People chattered to us in the beautiful soft language we couldn't understand but whose tones seemed concerned and congenial.

"T-o-k-y-o," Rosie said. "See, this is Tokyo," she repeated to the citizens surrounding us, sweeping her hand across the city, smiling. And all of them repeated "T-o-k-y-o" and nodded their heads in complete agreement.

It didn't occur to either of us until much later that the map was Western, with Western street designations, and everything was written in English, which most Japanese then could not read.

All of a sudden a man dressed in a tuxedo appeared from behind an alley.

"*Mande, señoritas, a su servicio*. May I assist you?" he asked, curling a Salvador Dalí mustache.

And he did.

We thanked him and walked away to the *ikebana*, bewitched.

But that's the sort of thing that would happen when I was with Rosie. She wasn't magical herself, she just beckoned magic.

The first time I saw her was at a bar in the small village of Placitas, near Albuquerque, New Mexico. The perfect hippie, on the run from a family far away. We were all from someplace else, our parents were all terrible, and we weren't old enough to forgive them yet. That ease of hers I was telling you about was immediately evident. A thick black braid hung down her back like an Indian princess, and her green fiesta skirt swayed to the Rolling Stones' "Honkey-Tonk Woman." She laughed and mingled with the regulars and spoke with a deep Southern drawl. I heard her ask the bartender for water, but it sounded like *warter*.

"What's that?" he pretended to misunderstand.

"You know, what you never mix with *awl*, honey," she said.

Rosie never drank, she used the bar, as we all did, like a community center, a general store, and her swimming pool eyes, clear now as they were then, caught mine several times. I wanted her for my friend, though I couldn't have told you why. I just knew in the surest way anyone knows, through my instincts. If you stare at someone you're attracted to long enough, and they look back, and that look is finally returned in the way first you gave it, you're bound to meet.

Unlike some friendships that go in and out of shine like the stars, Rosie and I got closer over time. She was the one to move to California first and I followed. We lived on the cheap in those days before Ronald Reagan legislated greed. Rosie was a junkyard angel, with fabulous vintage clothes and furniture she'd pick up at flea markets. There were children, there were romances, there were private accomplishments. But once life dealt us that thing called full-time jobs, we wound up in the same industry together, selling our wares, so to speak, one often getting the other work in the same company. It wasn't always smooth between us—there were small jealousies and petty competitions that over time faded. When we walk down the street together, men and small children smile at her instantly, not at me, because I don't smile easily. We're opposites, in fact, in most every way. But we've spent a lifetime talking, our topics are encyclopedic. We can chatter about lipstick and hair and the next minute switch to foreign policy. Sometimes after dinner, we'll talk so long on the phone, we can't do anything but say goodnight and each separately drop into bed to sleep, immediately.

You're thinking, about her decision to move away—it can't be that bad. After all, air travel is as common as a second-class bus ride in Mexico. And the telephone—you need to chat that much you can call each other every day, like Oprah calls her best friend halfway across the country. There's special rates for cases like yours. Or for God's sake get an 800 number.

Well, a friendship only works partly by ear. And it's just not the same when you have to visit someone from a long distance. A person, a body is part of a place, *is* the place. And no amount of urban advantage, of fancy food, great bookstores, foreign films, the cutting edge of everything from tattoos to architecture, horticultural miracles and reproductive technologies—nothing can make up for one person.

For a long time, Rosie has been this place for me. I don't have any other home.

Before things got out of hand with her thinking she might move away, we took our last business trip together. I'd like to think we visited my hometown, but how can you say that about Los Angeles, a site so unhomey, so evasive of nostalgia that it won't let you feel sentimental for as long as it takes a red light to turn green. You drive up to where you remember a restaurant used to be, where you'd neck with your high school sweetheart in between bites of grilled-cheese sandwiches and french fries, and you can almost smell the Aqua Velva cheap and sexy on his seventeen-year-old neck. But the restaurant is torn down. Replaced by a copy store, or a pink-and-cream-colored mini-mall with a video palace and shoes for under twelve dollars. I pass by my old high school and it's completely rebuilt and surrounded by a fourteen-foot-high security fence. The only thing the contractors left was the "rotunda" in the middle, which you can't see from the outside. Why, I once tried to take my husband to my old family house in the San Fernando Valley and the lawn had disappeared into a parking lot and the Spanish-style stucco front with arches and tiles was completely plastered over. Where was that old apricot tree across the street, the one some neighborhood boys tried to hang my brother from? There were apricot trees all up and down the block, we swung from them, we hid in them, we picked their fruit in late August. And got yelled at when we woke in the middle of the night with the runs.

I could no sooner imagine chopping down an old fruit tree that showed no signs of ill health than I could saying goodbye to my oldest friend.

I took Rosie to visit my parents, whom after all these years she'd never met. Not like she could meet my father, in the truest sense of the word, but I took her to visit him anyway at Hillside Memorial Park, where Al Jolson is buried too. Jolson's the main attraction, stuck up on a steep hill like a holiday centerpiece in the middle of the park, his golden crypt prominently visible from the freeway.

Thousands of people visit the grounds every day just to catch a photograph of the blue tiered fountain that flows from Al Jolson's mausoleum.

My father was an immigrant, always dazzled by spectacles, and Al Jolson was an immigrant, so I figure they're resting together eternally in the right place.

"Look," I pointed out to her as we climbed the Path of Everlasting Peace to find my father's plot.

"It's the one with the MD buried at the foot of the row, just in case," I said.

Rosie wasn't afraid of laughing in a cemetery. For decorum's sake, she turned her head a bit downward, switched to a solemn face, and smiled with her eyes, in solidarity.

Even though she'd been around the block a couple of times, done some things her own mother screamed and yelled about, she was still the kind of person you wanted to bring home to *your* mother.

"So you knew my daughter who never visits me from so long ago?" my mother lifted her head from her pillow. My mother is on her last legs, won't travel, never leaves the house, but she's been that way for twenty years and will probably live till she's a hundred and fifty.

"Yes, we've known each other since Vietnam."

It's funny to hear a country stand in for a whole era, but that's how we spoke. We'd often drop the word "war," just like the generation that came before us would say "Korea" and everyone would know what it meant.

"So Rosie since Vietnam, you marched together?" my mother queried, her eyes squinting suspiciously, as though marching together was like sleeping together. But my mother had it almost right, it was that intimate. She, like millions of parents, was against the war, but disapproved of her children exhibiting themselves in public about it.

"Yes," Rosie smiled a smile that would stop a killer, "and we're still marching."

When Rosie finally got laid off from S & M, she went on unemployment. Even though I was used to her deep optimism, I thought there was something eerie and ominous in her hopefulness, as though the job had been holding her and now unmoored, she was about to fly. She began to send out letters of application to all sorts companies in the South. They say a good salesperson can sell anything, but going from microchips to dog kibble borders on the desperate.

"I'm fed up and poor again," she laughed. "But you know, I kinda like living minimal. Thank God for rent control. I go to the movies on Tuesday nights for two dollars and fifty cents. I'm using the library again. I'm taking long walks. And I've got my potatoes, you know I love my potatoes. And while I'm waiting, I'm going to read a lot of books. And I'm going to break up with that no-count and my life is about to change."

She broke up with the dessert-no-main-course man.

She had three yard sales and enjoyed them.

She started combing the consignment shops and put outfits together that Milan couldn't rival.

And because she's a beautiful woman with an open heart, she ran into an old friend who used to coach her son's soccer team. They went out a couple of times, and in a few weeks, fell in love. I liked him instantly because he apparently had no plans to leave the area, though in those economically miserable times, the sight of two happy smiling people over thirty bordered on the insufferable.

She called everyone she knew and told them she was looking for a job, took up weight lifting, and went about her business.

Some mystics believe if you are unhappy with your life, change one small aspect of it and something new is bound to happen.

For months, she waited for word from all the jobs she'd applied for. Her new romance evolved into a nightly event. She had more faith than any woman I know, but the country was in the middle of a terrible recession and jobs were scarce. It got so bad that her teenage daughter would bring in the mail, fling it on the kitchen table and sigh.

"Anything for me, dear?" Rosie would ask hopefully.

"Nah," her daughter would say, "unless you count the Safeway coupons."

It's useless for someone like Rosie to worry about the basics. They fall into her lap, whether she wants them or not. Dressed to the hilt in one of her postmodern ensembles — new consignment shop sling-backs, a black leather miniskirt, and an oversize designer T-shirt — she met a man at a party who needed a project manager. She wound up with an easy commute and full benefits. And though we both know every job in this world is a stay of execution, it's what happens in between coming and going that matters.

No, the South did not rise again. Not in that way for Rosie, at least not imminently. And since I'm a hard-core Yankee, I'm rather happy at this recent and fortunate reprieve.